P9-EEG-891

Lambing Out

Lambing Out and other stories

Mary Clearman

A Breakthrough Book
University of Missouri Press
Columbia & London, 1977

University of Missouri Press, Columbia, Missouri 65201
Library of Congress Catalog Card Number 77–274

Library of Congress Cataloging in Publication Data

Clearman, Mary, 1939-
Lambing out, and other stories.

(A Breakthrough book)
CONTENTS: Lambing out.—The reining pattern.—The cat killers.—On the hellgate.—Paths unto the dead.—Slightly broken.—Monsters.
I. Title.
PZ4.C62265Lam [PS3553.L39] 813'.5'4 77–274
ISBN 0–8262–0227–6

"Lambing Out" originally appeared in *The North American Review,* Summer 1970. It was reprinted in *Prize Stories 1972: The O. Henry Awards.*

"The Reining Pattern" originally appeared in *The North American Review,* Winter, 1971.

"The Cat Killers" originally appeared in *The Iowa Review,* Winter, 1972.

"On the Hellgate" originally appeared in *Four Quarters* © La Salle College, 1974.

"Paths unto the Dead" originally appeared in *The Georgia Review,* Summer, 1974. It was reprinted in Martha Foley's *The Best American Short Stories: 1975.*

"Monsters" originally appeared in *The North American Review,* Winter, 1974.

for my grandmother
Mary E. Welch

Contents

Lambing Out

Lambing Out

The weather forecast had predicted that the snow would come in scattered flurries, but instead it began to fall steadily to create a deepening blanket over the hills and fences and last year's dead grass. There was no wind, and the snow fell straight down without letting up or increasing all through the day. It fell in a dull rhythm as though no power could make it alter, and what it touched it silenced. By three o'clock it had so darkened the world that the fence posts and telephone poles and occasional cattle drifting ahead of the storm were dim shapes through the white falling curtain, and lights from the scattered ranches were beginning to wink between the shrouded hills and the snow-filled sky. The snow flakes glistened in the reflection of the lights, and kept falling.

The snow was still falling when Nettie Evan got off the school bus at the gate by the barn. She stood out of the way while the bus groaned and spun in the snow and finally lurched back down the road. Its taillights shone briefly through the snow and were gone. Nettie turned to the gate. The milk cows were waiting to get into the barn, their shaggy winter hair crusted with snow that had melted from their body warmth and frozen again. Nettie pushed a deep swath through the soft snow with the poles of the gate and let the cows lumber ahead of her with their eyes bulging at the snow and their heavy udders swaying. The snow was capping the corral poles and banking against the house.

By the time Nettie had reached the house, her scarf and wool coat were crusted with snow and it was so dark that she could not see the hills that rose up around the huddle of buildings. The willows in the yard were snow draped and ghostly, and a yellow light beyond them marked the lambing shed. Nettie stopped and looked at the falling snow for a minute before she went inside. It had a monotony that deadened the senses just as it muffled the hills and ranches and even the moving creatures in white. The same flakes seemed to be falling over and over into the growing depth. Nettie thought of the weather forecast they had heard on the radio that morning, and how her father had silently eaten his breakfast and then gone out to look at the ewes that were waiting in the lambing shed. This snowfall was so steady that it might go on for days. Already the snow was six inches deep. There had been no wind today, but if the wind should rise in the night, the snow would drift and the roads would be blocked. Nettie looked down at the schoolbooks in her arms, the senior lit. text and the geometry book with the assignment marked. She would probably not get to school in the morning, and the class would be ahead of her again. Holding her books in one arm, she brushed the caked snow off her coat and scarf with the other and opened the kitchen door.

The heat from the coal range hit her face as she kicked the door shut behind her, and with it came a stench that she could not identify. The kitchen was dark, even with an electric light burning in the ceiling. Nettie's mother was hunched at the kitchen table with an empty coffee mug in front of her, staring out at the snow, and her little sister was squatting down in front of an apple box in the corner by the stove. Nettie set her books down on the oilcloth and untied her scarf. Her hair was limp and damp under it.

"Look what we got, Nettie," said her little sister. Her eyes were dark blue above her chapped cheeks. Nettie hung her coat and scarf on a nail by the door and went around the roaring stove so that she could see into the box.

"So that's what smells!"

There were two lambs in the box, limply splayed against one another. Their minute hoofs were yellow and rubbery and their eyes were closed. At first Netti thought they were not breathing, but when she looked closely she saw the rise and fall of the woolly sides.

"So the lambing's started," she said. "Fine time to pick."

At the table her mother stirred for the first time. "Damn good thing he got coal yesterday," she remarked, and fell silent again. Nettie looked around at the unswept kitchen, at the egg-smeared dishes stacked in the sink, and at her mother's heavy back stretching through her soiled house-dress. It was the snow, Nettie thought. Through the kitchen window, the flakes seemed to be spinning. She looked down at the sleeping lambs. The flour sack on which they lay was stained with yellow mucus.

"They're scoured," she said.

"What's scoured?" asked her sister.

"Their milk doesn't agree with them. Makes their bowels run. What kind of milk did they have?"

"Just milk."

"It'll have to be boiled, or they'll die."

The little girl sat on the edge of the box, looking down. Her matted fair hair was almost white in the light. "They're bums," she said. "Twins. We're going to feed them with a bottle. And I can play with them."

"If they live," said her mother from the table.

"Where's Dad?" Nettie asked. Her mother sat staring out over the coffee cup as though she had not heard. The falling snow spun in the light from the kitchen window.

"Out at the shed," said the little girl. "He went to water the sheep and see if more lambs come."

"Guess I better go help."

The child got up. "Can I come?"

Nettie looked down at her. Her denim overalls were torn and a thin knee protruded. "You'll have to put on some different clothes," Nettie told her.

"Told you to change your pants this morning, Sylvie," said her mother without turning away from the table. "You've worn 'em for a week."

"Come on," Nettie said. "I'll help you. But hurry up. Poor Dad's carrying water all by himself."

Her mother threw her chair back from the table, making Sylvie jump, and stood up. Carrying her coffee cup with her, she crossed to the stove and filled the cup from the pot. Her hand was shaking, and the coffee spattered and skittered in drops across the top of the range. "I knew these goddamn sheep were a mistake. Too old, for one thing. And he don't take care of 'em right. But you can't tell him—" Returning to the table, she sat down heavily and slopped more coffee on the oilcloth.

Nettie took her sister by the hand and led her up the kitchen stairs to the room under the eaves that they shared. She found an intact pair of overalls for Sylvie and helped her change. Then she hung her own school clothes behind the curtain that served as a closet and took down her blue jeans and a darned sweater. As she pulled the sweater over her head and straightened it around her hips, she caught sight of herself in the cloudy mirror that hung over the bureau. The girl peering out at her was anxious-eyed and muscular, with strong legs and thighs under the blue jeans. Her hair was limp. Nettie touched it, thought of taking time to comb it, and changed her mind.

"Come on, Sylvie, get your jacket."

By the time Nettie had bundled up her sister and started her out the back door, the tracks that she had made coming home from school were nearly filled with snow. The flakes were still falling in rhythm, but now that it was completely dark, they seemed more erratic. Nettie could feel them on her face and seen them whirl in the square of light that fell from the kitchen window. Sylvie stepped high and spraddle-legged, for the snow was nearly to her knees. She put out a hand and caught a few flakes on her mitten, put them to her tongue, and tasted.

"Ugh."

"That's your mitten you taste. Wet wool, silly."

Sylvie ran ahead toward the lambing shed, kicking up the snow as she went, then turned and ran back to her sister. The snow had frosted her scarf and sparkled as she turned up her face.

"I like the snow!"

"That's because you haven't been out in it long." Nettie stopped at the water trough outside the shed and filled the pail that she found there. The water dissolved the snow that had collected in the bucket and splashed on the ice around the trough as Nettie lifted it out and let her left arm swing out to balance. Sylvie frisked ahead of her, glad to be out of the house.

"Sing!" she called back to Nettie.

Lambing Out

"Sylvie say she love me, but I believe she lie—"

Nettie pulled the shed door open, maneuvered through with her pail of water, and blinked for a moment in the light. The shed was a little warmer than it was outside, but the chinking was falling from between the old logs and the snow was seeping through into the straw bedding. A dirty light bulb burned in the ceiling, where more wisps of straw hung from the reinforcing lath and chicken wire. Straight ahead of her was an aisle between the pens, and at the far end her father was leaning over and watching a ewe, his foot cocked on the bottom board of a panel. He looked up and saw Nettie.

"I got all that side watered. You might start down the other side."

Nettie turned to the first pen. The ewes were separated by rough board panels that could be wired together in different arrangements, depending upon the need. Now they were joined to make individual cubicles for the waiting ewes. Nettie lifted her bucket into the first pen and poured water into the trough. The ewe in the pen backed away and stamped her foot, yellow eyes looking through Nettie, wool caked with filth. Nettie half emptied her bucket and went on to the next pen.

Her father was still watching the ewe in the end pen when Nettie had filled all the remaining troughs and had hung up the bucket. He shot a look at her as she came to stand beside him, his eyes blue pinpoints in a grizzled face. He rubbed his bristles and turned back to the ewe.

"She going to lamb?" Nettie asked, to give him an opening.

He spat tobacco juice into the straw. "When she gets damn good and ready."

The ewe stopped pacing in her pen and backed into the far corner. She stamped, fidgeted, and stamped again. Her water was untouched. Nettie leaned on the panel, looking at the white-ringed yellow eyes that were fixed on a point far beyond her. The pupils were oblong and dilated, giving the ewe a wild, malevolent look. Nettie wondered why a sheep's eye seemed to hold so much concentrated and scheming evil when the truth was that the sheep was the stupidest of animals, too stupid to scheme anything.

Her father shot her a look. "How's your mother?"

"She's not saying anything."

He leaned heavily on the panel and pulled down the brim of his felt hat. "Snow gets to her."

"Nobody likes it much."

"Well—" he spat again into the straw. "You got to be raised to it. Somebody raised in town like your mother, it gets to them."

Nettie watched the ewe. Behind the sheep, where the log walls rose up out of the straw bedding, the bank of fine snow was growing. There was a sifting, then a trickle, and then a gust. Nettie's hand closed on the rough grain of the panel. Far outside the shed and the limits of the bare light bulb, a sound was gathering momentum, howling in the pines high up the ridges and swooping over the crests of the hills until, as though at its climax, it hit the north wall of the lambing shed. The old logs creaked, and more snow gusted in. The ewes were edgy, heads high and eyes wild.

"I should of got up to the haystack today," said Nettie's father.

Nettie stared at him. "How much have we got?"

"Enough for tomorrow."

"Can't you get up to the stack with the tractor?"

"Hope so."

The shed door opened, and Sylvie shot in on the crest of a wave of snow and cold air. The sheep jumped at the disturbance, lurching in their cubicles. Sylvie's nose and cheeks were red, and her dark blue eyes gleamed. "The wind!" she cried. "It blew me over in the snow!"

"Easy!" said her father. "You've scared the ewes."

Sylvie paid no attention to his caution, but ran panting up to them. Her scarf had slipped back and her fair hair rose up over it. Snow was sticking to her eyelashes and melting in her hair, and more snow was crusted up and down her leg and shoulder where she had fallen. She was hopping in excitement.

"You look like a snowman," Nettie told her. "A snow girl."

"She ought to learn to mind," said her father. He hunched his thick shoulders under his coat and darted look at Nettie. "No school for you tomorrow?"

"I don't suppose. Not with this wind."

His eyes roved over the nervous ewes. "Guess there'll be nothing doing till after supper. May as well go in."

"Sure."

"Just as well you'll be home a few days, the way your mother feels. Damn weather gets her down."

With Sylvie prancing ahead of them, Nettie and her father walked between the rows of sheep to the door. The wind whipped snow into their faces as they went out, and Nettie saw that there was already a drift running parallel with the lambing shed. More snow lifted like white smoke across it; then her father switched off the shed light and there was only the wind driving them through the darkness toward the yellow patch that was the kitchen window. It howled and sprayed them with hard grains of snow, and then slammed into their backs with all the force it had gathered in its career over the faraway ridges and empty plains, and only by walking stiff legged with their backs braced could Nettie and her father, with the child between them, keep from being driven into the snow.

Nettie cooked supper on the coal range and washed the dishes afterward while she boiled milk for the lambs. Her father went out once to check the ewes again and came back in with a gust of snow and the news that there were no new lambs. The wind did not let up, but banged and rattled around the eaves of the house. Its high whining note was far away, an undertone of the true noise of the storm, but Nettie found herself listening to it with her teeth biting hard together.

Sylvie listened to the wind with her eyes gleaming. The storm seemed to excite her. Nettie was pouring milk into a clean beer bottle when the little girl began whirling around and around in one spot, her head thrown back and a high squeal like the wind's coming from between her teeth.

"Stop it!" cried Nettie. She spilled milk over the lip of the full bottle and reached for the dish cloth. Sylvie stopped and stared at her sister.

"Bad enough to hear it outside without her screeching

in here," remarked their mother. She went on through the kitchen and into her bedroom with her bathrobe hunched around her.

Nettie looked at Sylvie's face. "Come on. You can help me feed the lambs," she offered.

Armed with the beer bottle of boiled milk, Nettie sat down on the edge of the apple box and got the biggest lamb under her arm. It did not resist having the nipple shoved into its mouth, but let its eyes roll back while the thick milk dribbled from between its gums and over Nettie's arm.

"Why isn't he hungry?" asked Sylvie, squatting by the box.

"Hasn't got sense enough, I guess." Nettie clamped the limp body between her leg and elbow and used the fingers thus freed to massage its throat. The lamb gulped and choked, and Nettie took the nipple away. "Guess maybe he swallowed some that time," she said, and forced the nipple into the lamb's mouth again. Working the bottle back and forth, she tried to tease the lamb into taking an interest in the milk.

"Let me hold the bottle," begged Sylvie.

"Guess you may as well." Nettie gave it to the child, but Sylvie could not keep the nipple in the lamb's mouth. Its head lolled on Nettie's leg and the milk soaked into her blue jeans.

"Maybe he drank a little," said Nettie at last. "Let's try the other one." She let the first lamb sag back into the apple box and got her fingers under the second, but it was cold.

"It's dead," she said, and set down the bottle.

Sylvie peered with interest into the box. "Why?"

"Oh, it just *is!*" Nettie tried to keep from snapping, but she felt tired. Her father got up and came over from his chair in the corner. He looked down at the two lambs, then bent and picked up the dead one by its middle. It dangled from his hand, four thin legs and a ropy tail. He crossed the kitchen unhurriedly and went out the door. Presently he returned without the lamb and went back to his chair.

The wind was still blowing when Nettie took Sylvie up

to bed. Up under the eaves, the storm seemed closer. The girls shivered as snow drove against the shingles and rattled on the loose panes. A curtain moved up and down, sank, and rose again with the blast. Nettie put Sylvie in bed and undressed herself in front of the mirror. Her hair hung lank on her neck and even though she knew that there would be no school tomorrow, she found her comb and bobby pins and began winding up the loose strands.

Somebody should do something about Sylvie's hair, she thought, and glanced at the bed, but the little girl was already asleep. Nettie jacked open the last bobby pin on her teeth, shoved it into her hair, and got into bed beside her sister. Her arms and shoulders ached from carrying buckets of water, and the quilts smelled musty. Sylvie turned in her sleep and rolled against Nettie, who turned to let the child settle into the curve of her body. Her sides rose and fell gently with the movement of the curtain. The wind whipped against the house. Nettie thought about Sylvie's hair. It should be cut, or at least combed. When Nettie had been Sylvie's age, her mother had fussed with her hair and kept it curled. But her mother was different now. Nettie stretched and let her eyes close.

The bang of the kitchen door woke her in the morning. She sat up in bed, shivering in the cold air and remembering the ewes. The bedroom window was frosted over and everything was still. It took her a minute to realize that the wind had died in the night. Then, tucking the quilts around the still sleeping Sylvie, Nettie got out of bed and crossed the floor with her bare toes curling. Snow had sifted through the loose window pane in the night, and she could see her breath. She found her sweater and blue jeans and dressed as fast as she could.

In the kitchen the range was roaring hot, and Nettie held her hands over it for a minute. Through her parents' door she could see her mother's bulk under the bedclothes. Nettie started a fresh pot of coffee and went to the kitchen window. It was frosted over in a glittering forest of ice crystals, and she had to scrape a hole before she could see. Even when she had a spot the size of her palm cleared, there was only whiteness, and she blinked.

"Oh lord!" she said aloud. Between the house and the

fence was a nearly level expanse of snow, but the wind had made a drift against the fence, or where the fence had been—Nettie was not certain, for the fence was invisible under the great flowing dune of snow, six feet high and running as far as Nettie could see.

"It still snowing?" her mother called.

"No. Guess it quit in the night. But you never saw such a drift."

Her mother did not answer, but Nettie heard the springs creak as she turned over in bed. The coffee pot boiled over and she went to move it to the back of the stove. When she did, she saw the lambs in the boxes, two in one box and one in another. One of the lambs might be the one she had tried to feed the night before, but even so there must be at least one more dead ewe and maybe two. Otherwise her father would have left the lambs with their mothers in the lambing shed. Nettie wondered whether they had been fed, or if she should boil more milk.

The kitchen door opened and her father came in, stamping the snow off his feet. There was more snow on his coat and collected on the brim of his hat. "Had to shovel my way out to the shed," he told her. "Let me have some of that coffee."

As Nettie poured him a cup, she saw that he had another lamb under his coat. He laid it in the second box and came over to the table to sit.

"You up many times in the night?" she asked.

"Two-three."

"Should have called me."

"Almost did, that last trip. Christ, you ought to see it out there."

Nettie wondered about the hay and the dead ewes. "Many lambs out there?"

"Four. That last one's a twin. The old bitch wouldn't claim him so I brought him in." He drained his cup and leaned over so that he could see through the bedroom door. "You going to get breakfast?"

"Sure."

"I'll take another look and be back in." He got up slowly and went out.

Before she started breakfast, Nettie went to the door and looked out. For a minute she had to squint, protecting her eyes against the glare of light on the snow. Then her pupils contracted and she saw that the whole world was sculptured white, broken only by the winding foxhole that her father had shoveled from the kitchen door to the lambing shed. He was just disappearing, shoulders brushing the top of his path on both sides. By standing on tiptoe, Nettie could see back toward the barn and corrals and the road. The wind had swept down from the hills across the whole expanse, driving the snow into elongated waves and drifts that skimmed up to the tops of the corral poles on one side and dropped off suddenly on the other. There was not a sign of life. Nothing moved. Even the leafless chokecherries below the barn were muffled in snow so that they could hardly be seen against the sweeping whiteness. Nettie shivered and went quickly back into the kitchen.

She made breakfast, fed her father and Sylvie, who came stumbling downstairs in her underpants with icy hands and feet, and boiled more milk for the lambs. By the middle of the morning, her father had brought in three more, but two of the first ones had died, and he carried them out to join the pile of frozen corpses on the south side of the shed. Her mother finally got up and sat in her bathrobe at he kitchen window, drinking cup after cup of thick coffee.

Sylvie moped about, resisting Nettie's attempt to comb her hair and taking an interest only in the lambs. She tried to play with them, but they were too young or too despondent.

"What's the matter with them?" she asked Nettie.

"I don't know. They're always like that. Guess they don't care if they live or die."

"I thought they'd be fun to play with."

"They are, when they get bigger."

"They're cute," Sylvie said and petted a head. She did not seem to mind the sour odor of milk and slime. Nettie herself was getting used to it, but she still thought that the lambs were repulsive, with their flaccid bodies and slack eyes.

Before it was time to start dinner, Nettie scrubbed the

boiled milk off her arms and tidied the kitchen and the cold front room. She straightened the chairs and dusted bric-a-brac and the photographs of the two little sisters who had died of polio before Sylvie was born, and then she sat down at the kitchen table to do her geometry assignment. She was very good at mathematics, even considering how much school she missed every year, but this morning she could not concentrate on the problems. At last she closed the book and got up to get dinner. Her mind kept wandering from the geometry teacher who said that she should go to college, to Sylvie's hair and whether she could cut it to look like anything.

In the late afternoon she helped her father feed and water the ewes again. There were several lambs in the cubicles now, and some of them were nursing and seemed to be all right. And there were some empty pens.

"How's the hay?" she asked.

"Enough for morning." Her father's eyes were bloodshot from the glare of the snow. When they came out of the shed, it was snowing again.

* * *

The next morning her father tunneled his way to the tractor and made an attempt to reach the haystack a half-mile away, but he ran into snow above the fenders before he was beyond the barn and had to abandon the tractor in a waste of churned snow.

"If we caught one of the horses, maybe we could get up there that way," Nettie suggested.

"Not with the hayrack."

"I mean, maybe we could drag down a few bales. Enough to get by on."

"Could be." He rubbed his bristles, considering, and spat tobacco juice in the snow. "Think you could catch old Pete?"

Nettie looked at him, at his bent shoulders and the grizzled folds about his mouth. "Probably. If I take some grain. You keep Sylvie with you?"

"All right," he said, and tramped off. Nettie went back to the house to get her boots and gloves. She followed the trail that was shoveled to the barn, and she collected a bridle and a lariat and a handful of grain. Then she struck off for the ridge where the horses would be hunting for exposed grass.

At first the snow was knee-deep, and she made fair progress, stepping high and breaking the crust only when she had to. Her breath steamed out in front of her, and she stopped twice to pant. Below her the drifts rippled down to the meadows and across the barnyard. She could see the shingles of the house where the heat had melted off the snow, and her father's square figure, shrunken by the distance, coming out of the shed door. From where she stood, the buildings and the tiny human figure were specks in a frozen sea. It was very quiet. She shivered and went on.

Near the top of the hill, she fell into a deep drift to her thighs and had to spread out on her belly to push herself out. Snow went down her neck and into her boots, and she thrashed until she found herself in knee-deep snow again. Ahead of her was bare ground where the wind had swept the snow from the crest of the ridge. She looked back at the churned snow. "Looks like a walrus went through there," she said aloud, to hear her own voice.

Once on bare ground her legs felt light and unencumbered. She walked north, swinging the wet bridle and stamping her feet. Across the gully on the upper meadow, she could see the haystack, a white-capped knob rising from the snow.

"Pete!" she called. "Pete!"

At last she felt something watching her and turned. Three horses were standing on a bare knob, eyes almost hidden under their winter fur, ears pricked toward her.

"Here, Pete!"

They did not budge, and Nettie swore. To reach them, she would have to wade through more snow. Holding the bridle and rope behind her, she swung off the ridge toward the horses. She would have to get by the two yearlings to reach Pete, and if the colts decided to run, he might follow. And she would never catch him.

"Pete!" she called, and held out her grain. To her relief, he stuck out his nose and came toward her with the two colts snorting behind him.

"That's a good Pete." He lipped at the grain in her gloved hand. Nettie fastened a bridle rein around his neck for insurance, then waited until he had eaten the grain. A few wet kernels fell on the snow as she slipped the bit in his mouth, and he nosed after them while she fastened the headstall.

"Hold still now." She got a double handful of mane and jumped until she had her belly over his back, then swung her leg over. His fur was warm under her thighs, and she could feel his ribs under the long hair. She nudged him with her boot heel and he moved off obediently toward the stack.

By picking her way, Nettie managed to get across the gully without floundering the old gelding. Once he broke through the crust to his belly and thrashed before getting back out, but they found shallower snow the next minute. At the stack, Nettie slid down and kicked the snow from a post before she tied Pete to it. She looked around. Last summer there had been a piece of corrugated tin along the haystack fence somewhere, if it hadn't rusted away. She walked along the fence, casting through the snow with her feet until she kicked the tin. Then she had to kick the snow away before she could get it out. She picked up the ten-foot length and pushed it up against the stack. It would hold about four bales, she thought.

She pushed two of the heavy, snow-weighted bales off the stack and then sat down to pant. The snow was seeping through the seat of her blue jeans, but she ignored it. Her hands hurt from hauling at the twine on the bales. All around her was snow.

Ten miles to the south, invisible now, would be the town and the school. She wondered if they were having classes, or whether the storm had closed the schools. A picture of the warm study hall came to her, and she saw the bent heads of the students, the clutter of books, and the whispers from the seniors as they talked about graduation and their applications for college. Nettie got up, dusted the snow off her rear, and tackled the next bale.

Once she had the bales on the strip of tin and anchored with the lariat, she felt more hopeful. She tied the other end of the rope in a bowline knot around Pete's neck and stood back to study her outfit. It looked all right. She climbed back on Pete and took up the reins.

"Okay, let's see what happens." Eyes on the hay, she nudged Pete into motion.

While they were on level ground, the hayload moved well, gliding over the crusted snow and making Pete snort and roll his eyes at it. The first trouble came when they started down off the hill, for the tin moved faster than Pete did and skidded into his hind legs, making him jump and shy. The tin sailed on by and came to a stop at the end of the rope. Pete's neck stretched forward, but he held fast.

Nettie urged him forward a step at a time. The hay edged downward for several feet, then overturned against a drift. Nettie slid down off the horse and waded through the snow to right it. Then they started down again.

They worked down by stages, while the afternoon darkened and the air grew colder. Nettie's fingers were numb on the reins by the time she finally reached the shed with her load. Her father came to meet her with his eyes on the hay. He untied the rope and pulled off the first bale.

"This'll get us through tonight," he said, then added, "There's a ewe down—think you could keep an eye on her?"

"Okay." Nettie unbridled Pete and let him go to stand under the shelter of the end of the shed. She wobbled and stamped her feet to bring the feeling back. Then she entered the shed.

Sylvie was sitting on the top of a panel with her nose running, looking down at the ewe that lay panting on the dirty straw. The little girl turned at her sister's steps. Her eyes were knowing.

"She's having a baby," she told Nettie.

Nettie leaned on the panel. Bedding was short and the straw was wet. Below it was the frozen ground and frozen sheep dung. The ewe strained, and saliva dribbled from her mouth. Nettie watched, hoping that things were going right, because she didn't know what to do if they weren't. Sylvie's eyes were solemn.

At the end of the shed came the familiar drive of the wind and a skiff of snow. Nettie's arms ached and her back ached. If the wind picked up again, if they got more snow, she didn't know if she could reach the haystack again. And there was only enough hay for the night. At her feet the ewe bleated, mouth against the straw, and heaved. Her sides worked. Slime ran from her, and then the rubbery front hoofs emerged with the lamb's wet head between them.

She heard her father banging a door somewhere and wondered if she should call him. It seemed all right, but she didn't know. The ewe's feet jerked twice, a bleat rattled from her throat, and she heaved again, hard. The lamb's body slid out on the ground.

"She had it," observed Sylvie.

The ewe raised her head, then put it down again. The lamb moved a little, but the ewe paid no attention.

"She ought to be mothering it," said Nettie. She took a gunny sack from the stack by the aisle, and stepped into the cubicle. Using the sack, she rubbed the slime and membranes from the lamb and cleared its nose of mucus. It squeaked and breathed.

"Watch out, Nettie!"

The ewe was on her feet, focusing her eyes on Nettie. Her head lowered. Nettie stepped aside, and as the ewe staggered up to butt her, kicked her on the side of the head. The ewe shook herself, trying to find another target.

"You old bitch, take care of your kid!" Nettie caught her by the ears and forced her nose against the lamb. "He's your lamb, you old fool!"

The ewe sniffed at the lamb. Nettie held her nose against it, wondering what she was doing wrong. Some ewes just never claimed their lambs. She scooped up the lamb and propped it against the ewe's hind legs, working the teat into its mouth. Then suddenly it was sucking milk and the ewe was turning to smell it. Nettie let go cautiously and backed out of the pen.

Her father appeared behind her. "Listen to that wind!"

Nettie turned. To her amazement, her father was smiling, cracked lips stretched away from his teeth.

"It's from the west. It's chinooking!"

Nettie and Sylvie followed him outside, and around the shed. The wind streamed against their faces and across the snow. Water was dripping from the eaves of the shed, and the great snow fields around the cluster of buildings seemed damp and shrunken.

"It must be twenty degrees warmer," said Nettie.

"That's that chinook wind for you," said her father. "We'll be knee-deep in water by tomorrow."

"We won't be able to get hay for mud."

"That's about right." Her father straightened. "We'd better get what lambs we can in the kitchen, or they'll die of pneumonia."

Sylvie followed them back and forth. The warm wind brought a more natural color into her cheeks and made her frisk. "What's a chinook?" she asked, and Nettie told her about the warm wind from the Pacific coast that dropped over the mountains and thawed the prairie states. Her father listened.

"Good thing for her you're graduating this spring."

That night Nettie went to sleep listening to water run off the eaves of the house, and in the morning the kitchen was full of damp and bleating lambs. Her father dragged more hay from the stack on the piece of tin, snaking it through soggy grass and mud, and they kept the ewes fed. The next day Nettie's mother got out of bed and dressed, and washed a load of sheets. Some of the lambs died of pneumonia, but some lived and frisked in the back lot where the snow had melted away from the rotted corpses of dead sheep. Sylvie caught an orphan lamb and sat in her swing with it dangling over her arm.

"I know where you came from," she told it, and sang the song that she liked Nettie to sing to her.

"Sylvie say she love me, but I believe she lie—hasn't been to see me since the last day of July!" Nettie sang when she drove the little band of sheep up to the spring pasture. She rode bareback on Pete, swinging the tin dogs ahead of her and making the sheep scurry away from the rattling cans. Sylvie with her hair matted in snarls and more wilful than ever was playing with the bum lambs back at the house. Looking over her shoulder, Nettie could see green grass cropping through the dead undergrowth and the last dirty patches of snow. The chokecherries were budding and magpies were nesting. Nettie had heard them squabbling over the carcasses of the dead sheep. Below her, her mother's wash flapped, and ahead of her the lambs ran and jumped straight into the air, careening

against their mothers and butting at one another. Some of them were the ones that she had forced to swallow boiled milk.

The wind stirred in the underbrush and ruffled Pete's winter hair that was shedding in handfuls over Nettie's legs. It penetrated her shirt, and she shivered, remembering.

The Reining Pattern

They attended the county horse show religiously, all the ranchers with gumbo still plastered to their boots and unpaid bills jammed in the jockey boxes of the pickups and station wagons and even Cadillacs that they parked in a circle around the racetrack. The townspeople, store owners, and the smattering of professional men and their families never came. The yearly ritual had nothing to do with them. They were uncomfortable about the whole show, nursing their own precarious sophistication and pretending that nothing was taking place beyond the city limits.

But the ranchers, whether they owned a mortgaged hundred and sixty acres or a mortgaged ten thousand, drove their pickups into a circle around the county racetrack, like Conestoga wagons drawn up against Indian attack, unloaded their horses, and watched one another go through the familiar drills and patterns. Each stylized movement was as jealously observed as the faith of their fathers.

The events—the cattle cutting, the breakaway roping, the fine reining—were anachronistic, designed by the grandfathers of the present contestants to show off the skills of working cowhorses and their own day-to-day life. Not even the big spreads worked cattle like that any more, although they sometimes pretended to. Nowadays they cut out a few yearlings every summer and fed them hay so that the kids could practice cow cutting. Ironically, the new strains of quarter horse and thoroughbred in the old mustang stock had developed a leggy, nervous breed that was far superior to the old working cowhorses. These new horses were trim and fast, agile as giant cats, and lived to compete in honor of a culture that had never quite existed.

Johnnie MacReady's four-year-old mare, for example. Johnnie and her father had trained her from a colt, groomed and fussed over her, and been jubilant together when she had taken best prospective stock horse three years ago. Since then, Johnnie had been working toward the advanced reining competition, the final and most prestigious event in the county horse show, and she had a mare that would have prompted her grandfather, fifty years dead but a top hand from Texas to Canada in his time, to have offered up his whole saddle string in trade.

Now at ten in the morning, as the wind brought the odor of cotton candy over the trampled grass of the fair grounds, Johnnie was passing up the pleasure-horse classes and grooming her mare in the shade of the horse barns. She ran the sponge of warm water over the beautiful thoroughbred legs, and the mare turned and nipped Johnnie's cropped hair.

"You're easy enough now," Johnnie growled, freeing her hair. The mare looked around at her comically. By afternoon, Johnnie knew, she would have all she could do to keep the mare's competition spirits under control.

The mare's head shot up, jolting Johnnie against the water bucket. "What the hell—"

"Take it easy. It's just me." Marty Croyland sat down opposite Johnnie on an upended barrel, stretched his bow legs out, and began to roll a cigarette. Johnnie glared at him.

"Could of give me some warning." She stood up and wiped her hands on the thighs of her Levi's, new for the occasion. Sweat beads were furrowing down her sunburned face. "Christ, she would have to go and roll this morning."

"She looks all right," Marty reassured her.

"You're not supposed to smoke in the barns."

"I'm outside."

Marty had, indeed, dug a little bare spot with the toe of his boot, Johnnie saw.

Marty was slim, just taller in his exaggerated boot heels than Johnnie. His faded blue jeans were skin tight, making him look more fragile than he was, but Johnnie knew from experience that Marty was one person she could not bully. Turning her back on him, she picked up a curry comb and set to work on the mare's long black tail.

"How's your dad? Hand still bothering him?"

"Yeah, he can't do nothing."

"I talked to Jake," said Marty.

Johnnie stopped combing. "When?"

"This morning, like I said, remember?"

"I remember."

"He's going to need a man to run that lower spread of his, down on the river. There's a house down there, and Jake'll supply groceries."

The curry comb resumed motion. There were few enough jobs that a cowboy could get and support a wife, she knew. "You gonna take it?"

"Well—" Marty's voice dwindled. He propped his cigarette carefully on his knee and took off his hat. From where she stood, Johnnie could see the thinning patches of his sweat-dampened hair. Marty was ten years older than she was. Boys her own age sickened her. "Might beat forty a month from Dad," Marty finished.

"That keeps you in gas and beer."

"Yeah, well, I might want more than that."

Johnnie turned back to the bucket and dropped the sponge in the now clammy water. She dried her hands on the tail of her shirt and looked down at the tiny diamond on her fourth finger. The little stone looked dainty and foreign on Johnnie's hand, sunburned and scarred with torn and bitten fingernails. Like something some town girl might wear, thought Johnnie. Like her cousin Donna.

At least Johnnie was no sissy town girl to fuss around with hand lotion, she told herself, and shoved her shirt tail back into her Levi's. Marty was going to expect her to marry him, a small voice whispered. "Money isn't everything," she told him.

"No."

Johnnie scowled at the sun. "Well—I suppose that way, we could get married this fall," she began.

"Yeah, well, that's what I thought."

The faint wind between the horse barns increased, rattling a beer can into the weeds, and driving a scrap of tinfoil into a clump of dusty crested wheat grass. From the far side of the barns came the electronic garble of the loudspeaker. Johnnie wondered how far they'd come with the pleasure events. She hoped the wind wouldn't pick up by afternoon.

The mare's ears pricked and Johnnie turned. Her mother was crossing the stretch of faded grass between the barns and the parked circle of cars and trucks, a picnic basket over one arm.

"I'm not hungry," Johnnie shouted. She knew she was getting nervous and despised her weakness.

"You better eat something. Marty, tell her." Johnnie's mother, a massive woman perpetually short of breath, tugged her print dress down around her thick midsection. "We're gonna have lunch over there, under the trees by the road. You two come along."

Johnnie's lip thrust out. "I ain't hungry!"

"Marty," appealed her mother. "Seems like you're the only one, outside her dad, can make her see sense."

"You better eat," Marty advised. "You'll just get more jitters if you don't."

"Don't have jitters."

"You don't have to worry about your figure," her mother joshed her. "Not like me."

That, at least, was true. Johnnie was built like a sixteen-year-old boy, breastless and hipless, with long thin arms and legs. Her straw-colored hair was cropped short and her peeling skin was bare of makeup. Some women, even ranch women, fussed with their hair and hands and duded themselves up, instead of getting out and putting in a day's work, but Johnnie had always been enough her father's girl, anxious enough to keep his comfortable approval, to deny any betraying yearnings after femininity.

Her mother was thinking something of the same kind. "Seen Donna this morning," she remarked. "Should of seen her—all gussied up. She thinks she's somebody."

Johnnie considered her cousin Donna, her mind momentarily distracted from the coming competition. "Donna's a damn dude."

"She's getting to be one, that's for sure." Johnnie's

mother shifted the picnic basket on her substantial forearm. "Her mother ought to put her to work out on some ranch. Titters, carries on, enough to make you sick. Thank God you were never boy crazy."

"If Donna'd ever do a day's work it'd kill her."

"Says she's gonna be an airline stewardess."

Johnnie sneered. "Her?"

"Thought that'd get you."

"Donna's pretty enough," said Marty peaceably.

Neither woman paid any attention to this irrelevancy but gazed together out across the grass, past the race course and over the barren foothills beyond, up to the mountains that rose up in the blue distance and closed in their world. Enough world for Johnnie, who remembered the stories of the grandfather who had been a top hand and respected through the whole American West. And his father before him, homesteader and Indian fighter. Even now, with power wires crisscrossing the sky and the faint hum of traffic from the state highway, Johnnie could imagine how it must have been.

A faraway drone attracted her attention, and after a moment she saw the glint of silver against the blue sky. A big airliner headed for Spokane. Johnnie thought of Donna's plans and sneered again. Donna making a big fuss over high school graduation, Donna and her big ideas about airline school, Donna and her frightening softness that Johnnie dreaded like quicksand.

Johnnie had worked four years toward the reining pattern, drudging away in the hot sun while Donna and girls like her had fun. This was world enough for her, she thought again, and hoped violently that the grandfather she had never seen would have approved of her.

Johnnie ate lunch after all, trying to make her stomach stop turning. She squatted under an aspen and gnawed on a chicken breast while Marty told her mother and father about Jake's offer. Marty and her father fell into a discussion of grass yields, how much Jake's calves had weighed at auction last fall, how much hay he had sold off the river meadows. Marty elicited none of the stiff-legged hostility from Johnnie's father that he had shown to the one or two other ranch boys who had previously come sniffing around

Johnnie. Hipshot and gnarled himself, he seemed to accept Marty and his collection of unhealed wounds from his brief bronc-riding career.

"I never thought you'd want any of that lovey-dovey nonsense," Johnnie's mother told her. Then she asked anxiously, "You're not gonna get married this fall, are you?"

Johnnie shrugged. "Don't know." Marty was watching her out of the corner of his eye.

"Marty," said Johnnie's mother, breathing heavily, "what's your dad gonna do? He can't run that place of his without help, and with the price of hired help the way it is—"

"I dunno," said Marty. "I don't know if he can make out alone, but still that place won't support two families."

"Well, you can't just leave him in the lurch, not this fall."

"It's a damn shame," began Johnnie's father, stretching back oratorically from his meal, "it's a damn shame there ain't no way a young man can support a family on the land any more." He glared around the little group. "By God, it used to be, maybe we didn't have so much, that was back in the 'thirties, but seemed like we got along all right. No electric bill, because we didn't have no electricity, no gas bill to speak of, just a little hay to winter the work teams—"

"Well, I sure wish you two could plan on gettin' married this fall," finished Johnnie's mother. "One thing, you're neither of you like some folks, thinking about nonsense all the time so's you can't wait."

"—No goddamn tractor repairs. Whole country's gone to machinery, hard to believe time's gone by like it has. And here's Johnnie just a kid still—"

Cries of greeting behind them made them all turn. Johnnie's uncle strode up to the little group, beaming over his embroidered Western-style shirt and dogger tie. Johnnie's father struggled to his feet, his infected hand to his stiff back, and Johnnie, seeing her aunt and the despised Donna straggling behind, threw her chicken breast into the weeds. Nervous as she was, and then have to put up with that bitch.

The men were shaking hands. If they had once shared a family resemblance, it was gone now. Johnnie's uncle had grown up on the old ranch, but the depression had sent him into a job in the county land office, where he had grown comfortable. Afraid of getting his hands dirty, as Johnnie's mother often said.

Her mother was turning to the women now, beaming falsely. "You all set for school this fall?" she asked Donna.

"It doesn't get started for another month," explained Donna.

"She's really looking forward to living in Spokane," Donna's mother rattled. Johnnie writhed. Prissy, butter-mouthed Donna. She could remember when Donna liked to get out and ride with the best of them. Not any more. Johnnie's resentful eyes moved over her cousin's blonde bob, her eyes set too close together, the sandals that exposed pink-painted toenails. Donna smiled at her, and Johnnie turned up the corners of her mouth unwillingly, wondering if Donna was making fun of her. The bitch. Bet she liked the boys to slobber over her.

"Johnnie thought about goin' on to school two years ago," Johnnie's mother was running on.

"Like hell," Johnnie growled. "I don't need no phony school to teach me what I want to know"

"When are you going to get married?" her aunt asked her.

"They'd like to get married this fall, but it don't look like they can," Johnnie's mother hurried. "Marty's father can't spare him, and you know the size of that place of his. Not big enough for two families."

Her aunt was clucking, commiserating.

"Maybe in another year, things'll look better," her mother went on. "One thing about Johnnie, she's in no killin' hurry. Don't know what her dad would do without her. She's always been his girl. Or boy. They just keep me around the place to cook."

Johnnie's father had caught the last of that. "Shame there ain't no way a young man can support a family on the land these days," he began again, lecturing his brother, who squirmed. "God damn it, they got you comin' and goin'—"

"There's jobs to be had—"

"In town, maybe. All right for some city guy."

"Donna and me, we're gonna take in the canning exhibits," said Johnnie's aunt. "Why don't you two come along? Wilma, Johnnie?"

"Well—" began her mother. Johnnie sprang up. The jitters were worse than they had been all morning.

"Christ! I ain't gonna waste no time on any goddamn canning exhibit!"

She strode off, liking the grate of her new Levi's rubbing thigh-to-thigh and her mother's nervous explanation: "Johnnie's got to see to her horse, she's riding in the reining competition this afternoon, and her dad ain't been able to help, what with his hand—"

Marty found her down at the barns. "Feel any better?"

Her hands were shaking, and she gnawed a nail. "I don't care! That dirty little bitch!" Johnnie wiped her forehead with the back of her arm, leaving a dirty streak and several strands of hair standing straight up. "What makes me the maddest is, she's my own cousin. And she don't have any more feel for what's important than—than some city dude. Thinks she's so smart. She just wants to get laid. Pink toenails! You notice that?"

"Well—" Marty mused a moment, taking off his hat and letting the breeze pick at the thin strands of hair. "Her folks brought her up to have things. Clothes, you know, make-up. Junk like that. She's just what she thinks she ought to be."

Johnnie sniffed hard. Her eyes were filling with tears that welled incongruously in the boyish face. "She's just like the rest of them girls I had to go to high school with. Shameless hussies!" Johnnie, who had been inside a church perhaps twice in her life, ended her jeremiad.

Marty looked at his pocket watch. "You know it's two o'clock?"

"Jesus, is it?"

Knuckling her tears away, Johnnie led out the mare and threw the saddle blanket across her back. The mare sidestepped, and the blanket hung crookedly. "God damn it, look at her!" The tears were flowing again.

"Calm down," Marty advised. "She's pickin' it up from you."

In the end, Marty, limping slightly from the leg that he

had smashed up in the saddle-bronc riding three years ago, saddled and bridled the mare, checked the stirrups and cinch, and led her up and down while Johnnie cried in the shade.

"Think you can take her now?"

"I've got to!"

"You really want to win this, don't you?" Marty's expression was odd.

"More than anything!" Johnnie sobbed again, her face contracted. "I've been training for four years—"

Her father stumped around the end of the barn. "Bring her up, Johnnie, they're callin' for the reining class now."

Johnnie snatched the reins from Marty's hand and slung them over the mare's neck. The mare turned and butted at her in play, and Johnnie yelped.

"What the hell did Donna do that worked her up like this?" Johnnie's father asked Marty. "Johnnie's just a kid, bawls buckets like that—"

Marty shrugged. "Here," he told Johnnie. "Get your reins gathered up, and quit your bawling, and get on."

Johnnie glared at him through swimming eyes, but obeyed. Her ungainly body swung up on the mare and suddenly became graceful. Nudging the mare with a spur, she moved off on a trot toward the arena.

"She sure can ride," said her father to Marty.

"She sure can."

Once on the horse, with the powerful muscles rippling between her legs, Johnnie's tears dried. She rode with a faintly Indian look, slouched in the saddle, long legs making her a part of the mare. The wind streaked her cropped hair and passing ranch folk turned to stare at her. Johnnie joined the other contestants in line in the arena, feeling the sun on her back and sparing a thought for Marty, who was so patient and treated her like a decent person. Not like some of those boys, like her mother said, with their minds on nonsense all the time.

She sat her mare in line, watching the other riders go through their drill in honor of the form of ancestor worship they had all chosen, the intricate series of figure eights and cloverleaf turns, watching for the little failures that the judge ought to catch. A hard-mouthed sorrel gelding that widened the circles and refused to back on command, a little roan that wouldn't change leads.

Then Johnnie was spurring her mare and cantering into the hard-packed arena, seeing her parents and Marty watching from the hood of Marty's old pickup, the white of her father's bandaged hand raised. The wind had risen, puffing dust into her eyes and making the flag stream from the pole in the center of the race course. That, too, was as it should be. The wind brought the odor of sweat and horses, the faint gasoline smell from the parked cars, and a tang of its own. It was the horse show smell; she had smelled it every year from babyhood.

She could feel the mare's mouth on the bit as she lifted the reins and began the wide canter in the largest of the figure eights. The mare's gait was even, and Johnnie's body moved with the roll like a dancer's, shifted from one stirrup to the other on the outer edges of the circles to make the mare change leads.

A ripple from the circle of spectators told her that she had ridden a perfect figure eight. Johnnie's hands were steady on the reins now, and she tasted dried salt tears on her lips as she gathered the mare for the second of the large figure eights. Around and around, change leads, around, and then around again; that was it. Johnnie's lips were moving like a votary's as her body dipped and shifted almost with the rippling stars and stripes above her, carrying the mare through another perfect course. The reins barely touched the satin neck; Johnnie's knees and shifting weight did the directing.

Now the small figure eights, so tight that the mare had barely enough room to turn, and yet must hold her canter or be disqualified. Johnnie choked up on her reins and pressed in with the spurs.

"Ohhhhh!" It was a long murmur, drawn from the crowd by the mare's perfect rhythmic canter, around in the short circle, lead change, then around again.

Once more. Johnnie's breath was coming evenly. She was barely aware of the wind blowing dust through her hair. Thank God she had no breasts to jounce—one more time.

"Ohhhh!"

Again the unbroken canter in a circle barely big enough to maneuver around, the change of leads in cramped space, the repeat around to the center of the figure eight. Johnnie halted the mare on cue, breathed hard, and faced the judge.

A nudge of the spurs, and three paces ahead. Then three paces directly back, Johnnie's mare not fighting the bit, but moving backwards as placidly as if it were her natural direction. As it nearly was, considering the hours Johnnie had spent on those reining patterns, over and over again in the corral until her lips were bitten raw and wind-chapped.

Back up. Pivot right, pivot left. Most horses hated to pivot.

Now the hardest part. The sidestep. Johnnie hesitated a fraction after the last pivot, her eyes on the mountains above the circle of cars, and what was almost a prayer on her lips. *Grandfather, let her sidestep, don't let her break forward. Please, Grandfather.*

She picked up the reins from the mare's neck. Let her sidestep. I've been a good girl. Four years and no nonsense, and after all, it's all I want.

Careful. Too much pressure one way or the other, and the mare would go forwards or backwards. Or turn. Now. The reins against the mare's neck, a series of little jerks, the spurs, lean far out to the side—there.

Daintily, lifting her feet high as if in distaste for the unnatural exercise forced upon her, the mare stepped sideways like a crab, hesitating at first, then moving with much more assurance sideways across the arena.

Another ripple of applause, growing louder, and Johnnie let out her breath. "Thanks," she whispered to some unknown ear. Easily then she rode the mare back to her place in line to watch the last two contestants. Marty was smiling at her from across the arena, but she did not look at him. *Not marriage,* Johnnie thought, *not stupid marriage after this.* She had won, she knew.

When they gave her the blue ribbon, she was thinking that her mother would suppose that she had won her over by argument. *But it isn't that, Grandfather,* she told herself.

Marty knew.

"Told Jake I couldn't leave Dad alone," he explained that evening in her father's kitchen.

Johnnie nodded, relieved. "Maybe next year."

The Cat Killers

Camp Sunnybank, where I spent a summer instructing twelve-year-old hoodlums in riflery, had been a little subsistence farm in central Missouri. An old couple had scraped a sort of living from it for years, but finally old age and arthritis, and maybe even an objection on their part to doing without central heat and electricity for the rest of their lives, got the better of them. They sold the farm to the city parks and recreation department for a day camp, and moved to town, leaving behind them a couple of unpainted sheds, a sagging frame house with no plumbing but with a hardshell Baptist look of withstanding the worst, and an old blue tomcat and three young cats, his descendants.

This part of Missouri is rolling hill country, soft land that looks tender in the spring. The farm was knee-deep in clover and timothy that hadn't been pastured for years, shaded by elms and old fruit trees and cottonwoods down by the creek. It was hard for me to stand in the farmyard under the old pear tree, look across those hills, and believe that two old people had just missed starvation there. My part of Kansas looks tough, and when I first came down to Missouri to college, I couldn't believe the lushness. But it's wheatland where I come from. This farm was too small and poor, and all the soft and tender grass was just a come-on. Even the pears never matured.

The farm was a good enough place for a day camp, though, only ten miles from town, and still wooded and secluded. A creek ran through the meadow and down through a series of limestone caves, and there were raccoons and opossums in the trees, and copperheads in the grass. We counselors, most of us college students hired for the summer, spent a week setting up a picnic area, laying out archery and riflery ranges, putting up a science center in the least dilapidated of the old farm sheds, and erecting a pair of outhouses labeled "braves" and "squaws." The elderly science counselor, a school teacher during the rest of the year, taught us how to recognize a copperhead, and we were set. I thought I had a soft job.

No kid was bitten by a copperhead, not during the summer I spent at the camp, though one parent came close to it. On parents' night, he came up to the science counselor carrying a small copperhead and wanting to know what kind of snake he'd found. Dudley, the counselor, who'd worn himself hoarse that summer making the kids leave the copperheads alone, was still quivering when he told us about it. No kid was ever bitten, as I said. We had a mean bunch of kids.

The first kids that came were mostly white, lazy, and fretful. Their parents had evidently seen the day camp as the ideal way to force their complaining children out of their air-conditioned living rooms for the summer. Then one of the counselors, Tony King, began dragging in kids from the federal housing project in town. Everybody referred to them as the "Project" kids, and they were black and mean. I don't know which group was worst, but after a day on the rifle range with my outfit, I understood how Dudley felt about the copperheads. Maybe learning to use a twenty-two rifle was good for their frustrations, but it was hell on me.

When I had time to spare from worrying about getting shot in the back, I used to wonder about the effect of those potential snipers and guerrillas and ordinary hell-raisers a few years from now, all trained in the use of small arms at public expense. Mostly I worried about me. I checked every kid at the firing line to make sure he'd ejected his shell from the magazine before I went down to retrieve the targets from the trees I nailed them to. All the way down and back my skin crawled.

My back was a tempting target, I knew, and sometimes I could almost feel the shell between my shoulder blades. The kids giggled and arsed around, and I sweated. It was three weeks before I thought to send one of the kids down after the targets while I kept the rest of the outfit from plugging him.

The kids flattened the grass all over the farm, drove the nesting songbirds to neurosis, fell in the creek, caught an opossum and managed to cage him in a garbage can for Dudley's science center without being bitten, and profited from their interrelationship. Which is to say, the black kids learned some sadistic new twists to their deviltry, and the white kids learned a lot of new words.

To do them all justice, nobody seemed racially prejudiced. When they tried to kill each other, they did it impartially. And most surprising to me, all the time they were goosing each other and stealing lunches and dropping spiders into each other's cokes and setting people's pants on fire and hammering on each other, they were perfectly cheerful. It didn't make any sense to me.

Even the kid that threw the axe at Tony King, the woodcraft counselor, and nearly took his leg off just below the knee was cheerful enough. I guess he just wanted to see Tony without one leg. Or hopefully, see how he looked dead. He wasn't mad about anything.

He wasn't prejudiced, either, as far as I could make out, because he was black (one of Tony's Project kids, in fact) and so was Tony. It was midafternoon, and I was just bringing my riflery squad back for cokes, when we passed Tony's woodcraft class and saw the kid lean over and pick up the axe. Tony had his back turned, showing another kid something about tree bark. I yelled, my squad cheered and brandished their twenty-twos, and Tony half-turned, saw what was going on, and jumped almost but not quite in time to get out of the path of the blade. It slashed a four-inch gash out of his Levi's and nicked the calf of his leg. The axe, when we looked at it later, was razor sharp, and why anybody'd honed it like that and turned it over to the kids, we never knew. It was like teaching them riflery. Unrealistic.

I scooped up Tony's kids with mine and took them all up to the farmhouse to turn the axe-thrower over to Mrs. Boswell, the head counselor, for a quiet talk, while Tony got old Dudley to doctor his cut. Tony limped for a couple days, but the axe-thrower emerged from the farmhouse after half an hour, draining a coke and looking pleased with himself. It would have saved everybody trouble—us, himself, society—to have taken him out and shot him. But Mrs. Boswell talked quietly with him, and gave him a coke. Even Tony, who you'd expect to show some resentment, didn't say much. He growled something about the little bastard and was careful from then on how he turned his back on the pack.

But I never understood Tony King. I didn't like him, really. My dislike wasn't anything I could explain, because anybody I tried to explain it to would have been bound to think it was because Tony was black and I'm white. I'm not prejudiced. There aren't any Negroes in my part of Kansas, I never even saw one until I started high school in the consolidated district, and then I always got along all right.

Tony was about twenty that summer, the same age as I was. Old Dudley told me that he was majoring in biology and was damned sharp at it, but Tony never said anything about it. He was lean and long boned, and he wore a college sweatshirt with the sleeves hacked off, and a frayed black cowboy hat pulled down over close-set eyes, and he had a shamble-hipped walk that the kids used to imitate. He never talked much, and he never did anything to me to make me dislike him. Except things that I took for granted, just common sense things that anybody would take for granted, seemed to irritate him. And I always sensed that he didn't like me.

He was the same way with old Dudley. Dudley's schoolteacherliness carried over into his day camp work, and he did his best to instill some sense of the future into his class of screw-offs, along with information on Missouri minerals and plant life, and, always, the copperheads.

"Look at Tony, there," Dudley would urge his snickering little circle. "Look what he's made of himself. All on his own, too. He climbed out of the gutter, and got through high school, and he's going to be a fine biologist some day." The speech was punctuated by blasts into his handkerchief, for Dudley suffered horribly from hay fever, and the time he spent out in the country was misery. The pay wasn't that much, either, but Dudley was an earnest old man who thought the work was worthwhile, so he sneezed and went on. Eyes watering, mopping at his nose, putting up with kids that dropped frogs into his hot coffee, never seeming to notice that he wasn't making a dent in their understanding. He reminded me of the old couple that had owned the farm, beating themselves to death against all that raw material and never changing it into anything productive. I couldn't see why it took them so long to learn.

Dudley, I learned, taught school in the small Missouri town where Tony had climbed out of the gutter all by himself, and I listened along with the kids to the biographical details that Dudley supplied, until one day I saw Tony listening, too.

It wasn't unusual to find counselors anywhere in that camp. I was on my way from the rifle range to the store room for some twenty-two shells, and Tony was shambling down from the farmhouse when we met outside the shed where Dudley conducted his science and character-building classes.

"Pay attention to Tony, now," Dudley was chattering from inside the shed. "See what he's made of himself. No reason why you can't do the same thing."

I turned around to Tony, grinning at Dudley's earnestness, but the look on Tony's face, even what I could see of it under the hat, ended my grin. For a minute I just stared at him, seeing the mosquito bite on his neck and the bramble scratch across his cheek where a scab was drying, and the beads of sweat trickling down from under the cowboy hat, and the way his mouth was twisted. I'd never looked at Tony like that, but just for a minute all I could do was to stare at that mosquito bite, while I realized that he disliked harmless old Dudley as much as he did me. I turned and walked off.

I didn't understand it, I still don't. Not really hate, but just plain dislike.

But while Dudley tried to improve character and teach the kids about the Missouri countryside and save them from the copperheads, and while I averted homicides on the rifle range, and while Tony King stalked around the woods teaching woodcraft with his hat pulled down over his eyes and not looking at anybody else, a new problem developed, and that was the cat problem.

The old folks had left the old blue tomcat and the three half-grown kittens behind when they left the farm. It would have been kinder to have shot them instead, but maybe they were sentimental, or maybe they just didn't want to bother. Whichever way, they abandoned the cats. During the early spring, when nests of baby cottontails and mice and songbirds were plentiful, the cats had done well enough. Gradually, though, we all noticed that the rabbits didn't seem as thick as they had been. I saw the old tomcat once with a lizard, and another time with a grass snake clamped between his teeth and writhing at both ends. The tom had apparently hunted the neighborhood empty, and his sides were gaunt under his fur. The kittens, less expert, looked even worse, with their hair coming out in patches and strings of matter collecting around their eyes.

Finally all four cats took to haunting the picnic grounds while the kids ate their sack lunches, waiting to pounce on bread crusts and cookie crumbs. At last the old blue tom got too hungry to wait for a crust and grabbed a sandwich right out of a girl's hand. The girl was too surprised to do anything but sit and stare at her empty hand, while the old blue tom carried the sandwich off to the bushes and growled over it.

Mrs. Boswell, who had seen it all, called Tony and me over after lunch.

"We've got to do something about those cats," she said, keeping her voice down so that the kids wouldn't hear. It's only a matter of time until one of them bites a child. And the kittens are sick. Have you noticed their eyes?"

We had.

"What do you want us to do?" asked Tony. He had kicked a little hole in the ground with the toe of his boot, and now he filled it up again. He seemed to like Mrs. Boswell, or at least not dislike her, which was strange, because she never had much to say to him.

"Well, they'll have to be killed," said Mrs. Boswell. "The humane society won't come clear out here, and, well, those cats are sick, you know. The humane society would kill them if they had them. You know that, Tony." I didn't know why she was making a point of explaining to Tony. He jammed his hands down in his Levi's pockets so that the cords stood out in his forearms, and said nothing.

"I can borrow a twenty-two rifle from the rifle range," I suggested.

"No," said Mrs. Boswell, "because I don't want to take a chance of your hitting anything else, Mike. Besides, one shot will bring every child on the run, and it's bound to upset them."

I could imagine those young hoodlums being upset over a cat being shot. Mrs. Boswell was right, of course, that a shot would bring them all running hopefully. Probably they'd set up a wail about the poor pussy cats, which would be completely phony. But I didn't say any more.

"Try to think of a quiet way to get rid of them," Mrs. Boswell went on. "Something that won't attract attention. I wouldn't ask you to do it, but—" she still had that peculiar apologetic note in her voice, and I looked from her to Tony. Tony had been putting in summers for the parks and recreation department for three years, I knew, even while they still camped out in the city park, so maybe Mrs. Boswell knew him better than I did.

"It's just that there's nobody else to ask," she ended. "Dudley, of course, and you know how he is. And those girls over in the arts and crafts center." She shrugged.

Tony nodded, and left his chin down so that his hat covered his face. "Well, we'll do something," he said.

She looked relieved. "I knew you would," she told us, and went off to supervise the shed where a pair of college girls were running a class in woodcarving and finger cutting.

I looked at Tony, and after a while he gave me a grudging glance and went back under his hat. "Well," he said, "hell. I guess we better catch 'em, first."

Catching the cats turned out to be the easiest step. We borrowed the opossum's garbage can, shutting the furiously snarling opossum temporarily under a water bucket weighted down with a stone, leaving him rattling his teeth all by himself and switching his naked tail out from under the rim of the bucket. Then we took the garbage can out in the bushes below the picnic grounds and laid it on its side. We baited the can with slices of lunch meat, and waited with the lid until the kittens came sniffing after the meat, then hurried out and clamped the lid down.

Two of the kittens were so sick that they could barely crawl into the can after the meat. I'm not sentimental about animals, or squeamish either. Farm kids usually aren't. But my stomach worked at the sight of those kittens, and I wished I hadn't eaten lunch. Their hair was coming out in bunches, and maggots had formed squirming pockets along their backs. Their eyes were half crusted shut with yellow slime, and fleas worked busily in that.

"Jesus," said Tony. "Think we can kill the poor little bastards without touching 'em?"

The idea that Tony liked their looks even less than I did, of Tony with his gutter antecedents showing signs of squeamishness, helped to settle my stomach. We both walked off a little way from the garbage can with the two kittens in it, and talked about ways to kill the cats.

The easiest thing would have been to shoot them, except that Mrs. Boswell didn't want us to, and then if we shot these two, the others might get suspicious. I'd done plenty of things to cats when I was a kid on a Kansas farm, but all of those things involved touching the cat at some point. We could have brained them with a rock, except that we didn't want to get that close to them, or we could have drowned them if the creek had been closer and we hadn't been afraid of poisoning the water. And people since have told me a whole lot of other methods that didn't occur to Tony or me that afternoon.

"Let's throttle the mothuhs," said Tony finally, his voice going thick on him. I watched the muscles in his neck.

"What do you mean, throttle 'em? With your bare hands? They aren't heavy enough to hang."

Tony gave me one of his bleak looks, not much diluted by his reaction to the sick cats. "I think old Dudley's got some clothesline rope."

"Yes, but—"

Tony treated my arguments as though they had come from one of the sick cats. He went shamble-hipping off to get the rope from Dudley. Finally I followed him up to the science shed, listened to the obligatory discussion, and followed him back down to the garbage can again with the length of rope.

Then he showed me what he had in mind. We tied a slip knot around the neck of the weaker kitten, taking pains not to breathe deeply as we did it, then both backed off with an end of the rope in opposite directions, and pulled. It didn't take long. The kitten scrabbled with its hind feet and rolled its eyes back, but it was too sick to struggle much.

The other kitten was no more trouble. I didn't exactly enjoy hauling back on my end of the rope and waiting until the cat stopped scrabbling, but Tony surprised me. Once, looking at him over the cat on the rope between us, I thought he was going to be sick. Old tough Tony, no less.

The last kitten was more trouble. We caught him easily enough, but he had been eating better than his brothers, and wasn't quite so sick. He backed up in the garbage can where we couldn't reach him without taking a chance on being bitten, and snarled.

"Little sonofabitch," I snarled back. Tony and I were both dripping sweat. It was one of those hundred-degree Missouri summer days. The humidity was so high that you felt as though you could dive and swim through the air, and the first two kittens were draped on a stump, waiting to be buried. The last kitten showed his tiny teeth at us, sweat ran through our eyebrows and into our eyes, and all the time we could hear the kids yelling from the farmhouse yard where they were playing volleyball.

Tony made a lasso in one end of the clothesline rope and made a trial swing or two with it.

I didn't like the looks of it. "What good's that going to do? You can't hang that cat, he's too light."

Tony glanced over his shoulder and gave me one of his not-looks. "You got a better idea, wise-ass?" He peered under the lid of the garbage can, and the kitten spat at him.

"Once you get it on him, you won't be able to get it off."

"God damn it, you got so much advice, you do it!" He didn't offer to give me the rope, though. Instead he turned the garbage can upright, waited until the kitten had frantically got its footing again, and started fishing with his noose. He made several bad tries, but at last he gave a jerk and the kitten came sailing out of the can at the end of the clothesline rope. I dodged out of its path as it made an arc through the air, lit in a clump of grass, spun to its feet, and was running before Tony could haul it in again.

"Now what're you going to do?" I yelled. The kitten, restrained by the rope from going any further in one direction, bolted straight for Tony and arrived at the end of the rope in the other direction.

"Told you, you couldn't hang him."

"Shut up, you bastard." Tony had shortened his hold on the rope and began doing what he'd apparently contemplated from the beginning, swinging the kitten on the end of the rope until its own momentum created enough force to strangle it. All I did was keep out of the way.

Finally he let the kitten down. I got the noose off its neck with a stick. It was dead, all right. I looked up in time to catch Tony bent over at the waist, puking into the bushes.

Nothing was funny about the situation, but I started laughing anyway. I stood there with the dead kitten at my feet, two more dead kittens being worried by flies on a stump, looked across at Tony lifting his head and turning gray around the mouth, and laughed.

Tony's hat was gone, and his eyes looked naked without its protection. "God damn you," he said. "You bastard."

I couldn't stop laughing. "You're goddamned tough," I told him. "You cool bastard! You can't even keep your lunch down over these damn cats. Lot of cool you got!" That was what amused me so, I guess, the idea of old gutter Tony losing his cool over what any farm kid had done at twelve years old.

But he was burning mad now. His hair was plastered flat with sweat where his hat had rested, and sweat was running down his neck and arms. "You dumb bastard," he rasped, wiping his mouth off with the back of his arm.

I'd got my laugh down to a grin by now. "I never figured you'd go all sentimental over a bunch of sick cats, anyway. I figured you had that much cool."

"Sentimental?" That stopped him in his tracks. He mouthed the word over, syllable by syllable, as if he didn't know what it meant. "Sentimental?" Then his eyes got tight. "You stupid, stupid bastard—listen, you dumb sonofabitch, you like it so well, you take care of that tomcat. See how you enjoy it. You bastard."

"Okay," I said, though I knew that the tomcat was wilier than the kittens had been, and in better shape, too. "Sure, I'll do it."

Tony found his hat and sat down under a tree. "Stupid, stupid," he kept muttering. "Stupid, stupid."

I wondered if the heat had got to him. The sun steamed down even through the leaves, and I had a burning circle of chigger bites all around my groin. But I had laughed myself into a corner, so I went ahead and rebaited the garbage can.

By the time I had the garbage can rigged again, Tony had stopped talking to himself. He leaned back on the tree, jacked his knees up, and watched me from under his hat with a cynical grin. I watched him, too, as much as I could without being too obvious about it. Tony's expression of foreknowledge worried me; he looked as if he knew I was going to find out something that he had known for a long time, and he was just going to wait under that tree until I found it out. He made me nervous. I kept glancing around to see if he still looked the same way. He did.

The old blue tomcat hadn't survived all this time for nothing. For a long time he wouldn't come near the garbage can, even when I'd moved it to a fresh spot and laid an enticing little trail of lunch meat from it out into the bushes. When he finally did come out to investigate, he took his time, looking at the scraps of bologna and then in our direction. At last he snatched a bit of meat and bolted it whole, glaring in our direction with his ragged fighting ears flattened. Then another stealthy advance on the next scrap of meat, another long hesitation.

I was sweating, and my chigger bites itched worse and worse as the afternoon wore on. Tony just sat there, a little way off, with a glint in his eye, while the tomcat stalked my trap and I chafed. That bastard Tony, I'd like to beat him to death, and that damned blue cat, too.

It took the tomcat nearly an hour to make up his mind to go after the meat in the garbage can. He must have had a good idea what I was up to, and it was only being so hungry that made him give in at last. He leaped into the garbage can, seized the meat, and sprang for the mouth of the can again. I was barely in time with the lid. The tomcat hit it and snarled just as I clamped it shut. I righted the can and sat on it, listening to the tomcat growl under me.

Tony waited, and I wiped an armload of sweat off my forehead. I was going to have to get the cat out of the can the same way Tony had, only the tomcat was going to be more to handle than even the healthiest kitten had been. Damn it, I didn't like it. I wiped my forehead again, and Tony still waited.

While I fetched the length of clothesline rope and pretended to tighten the lasso, I thought about the cats I'd tormented in my life, how I'd been through all this and it didn't mean a thing. The tomcat never stopped growling, a vicious steady rumble that echoed inside the can, and when I lifted the lid a crack, he leaped for daylight. I slammed it again.

I looked over my shoulder at Tony, opened the lid just a crack again, and again the tomcat leaped, never stopping his growl. He had a sick, rotten smell about him that the hot sun made worse, and my stomach lurched. None of that, I thought. I'd have to drape the lasso over the top of the can, raise the lid, and jerk like hell when the tomcat made his leap for freedom. If I missed him, I might never catch him again, for he'd be even warier after having been caught once. But what the hell? I didn't care if he bit and infected every kid in camp. All I wanted was to get it to hell over with, go home and take a shower, and put something on my chigger bites. The tomcat rammed against the side of the garbage can, and Tony waited under his tree, smiling with that been-there-before look on his face.

I got my loop just where I wanted it. The angry, rumbling growl wound on and on from inside the garbage can. One thing was for sure, I wasn't going to take a chance on being bitten myself. That old blue tom could roam the camp forever first. His smell seeped out and filled my throat, and I nudged my loop into just the right spot.

As the lid came up, the tomcat made his third leap, and it was a good one, sending him clear of the garbage can and hurtling toward the bushes in one motion. I jerked my loop, just a little too slowly, and the tomcat squalled three octaves higher than his growl. Oh, Christ, I thought, I had him around his middle instead of his neck.

The tomcat was rolling over and over, clawing at the rope with all four feet, while I ran to keep the slack out of the rope. Over my shoulder I saw him bounce on a rock and shoot several feet into the air. He came down clawing and spitting. I ran, choking up on the length of rope as I went, until at last I thought I had a short enough hold to be able to stop. I turned, and the tomcat whipped over on his feet and growled at me from three feet away.

Tony had left the shade and just stood there, his hands stuck down in his back pockets. "You can't strangle him around the belly." He leaned back and watched me from under his hat, waiting to see what I would do next.

"Screw off," I told him, "or else get a club and beat him to death while I hold him."

"Beat your own cat to death."

"Well, I can't keep him on this rope and beat him at the same time," I shouted. The sweat on my cheeks was partly tears, I was so damned mad at that cat and at Tony. And at myself, too. Screw them both, and the whole pitiful camp full of mean bastards of kids that would as soon kill me as not and that I was supposed to be protecting from sick cats.

I just had on tennis shoes. If I'd been wearing logger boots, maybe, I could have kicked the tomcat to death. But I was so mad that I didn't stop to think about my tennis shoes. I just shortened my hold on the rope and waded into the tomcat.

The first couple of kicks caught him by surprise, and he doubled up and tried to get away. The rope held him, though, and after those few frantic clawings away from me, he turned on me, wrapping himself around the leg that was doing the kicking, and burrowing in with all his claws and teeth.

I felt them through my blue jeans and yelled. The cat and I must have been going around in circles, because at intervals I saw Tony looking on. It was like watching your parents watching you on a merry-go-round, except that the cat and I were taking less time on cycles. Tony still had that wise look, but I didn't have time to think about Tony. I stopped turning around, stood on the leg the cat had, and kicked the cat with the other foot. He came partly unstuck from my leg, with shreds of denim in his claws, and I gave him a couple good chops in the belly before he attached himself again. By that time I was feeling no pain. I mean, I felt him shredding my leg from the calf to the ankle, but I didn't care any more. All I cared about was hurting that cat, and I kicked and kicked until all I could feel in the world was the sensation my toes got from driving again and again into that squirming, biting bag of fur and bones. Somewhere I heard a funny high-pitched voice, and dimly I thought it was Tony yelling, but he said afterwards that it was me, screaming at the cat. I didn't know it. All I knew was kick, kick, into that cat, the sweat, and how mad I was, and all that sweat and madness turning into pure pleasure in the kicking.

I must have let go of the rope. Because I gave one last kick, and the tomcat, trailing the rope like a tail on a kite, went sailing into free air. He went up and up, it seemed to me in slow motion, and finally began to come down. I don't know where he landed. He landed somewhere out of sight. I know he survived, because we caught glimpses of him through the bushes the rest of the summer, but I didn't know that at the time.

I stopped screaming and looked down at my legs. My blue jeans were shredded and blood-stained up and down. As I stood there, my heart stopped racing and gave a few big, hard, slow beats. I breathed out.

I looked up, and there was Tony. The been-there-before look was still on his face, but it didn't make me mad. Maybe I was too tired. I just felt, for once, as stupid as Tony had said I was. So that was what he knew, and why he hadn't wanted to kill the cats in the first place, and why he was so outraged when I laughed. He knew how it felt, and maybe he hated sharing the outrage with me.

I wiped my face and went to find Dudley and get some stuff for my legs where the tomcat had clawed me. Tony followed me up to the science shed. He never said a word.

He didn't say much to me for the rest of that summer. He had never had much to say to me before that. But from then on I knew what it was he didn't say, and that made all the difference.

On the Hellgate

Sam Butler enrolled in the University of Montana graduate school for a summer term, more or less by default. He had been bored with the teaching job he had held for one year, and had made only the mildest efforts to find another position. The army didn't want him because of a slightly stiffened knee from a fall in his childhood. His undergraduate grades weren't really high enough to get him into graduate school, but finally the dean wrote that doing well for a summer term might make a difference. So Sam bought an airplane ticket for Missoula and signed up for a course in Renaissance nondramatic literature and for a seminar on Poe, with an asterisk by his name that showed he was there on sufferance, cashed one of his mother's checks, and paid for fifty dollars worth of books and the rent on an attic bedroom a few blocks from campus. In the condemned section, as his landlady wisecracked when he paid her.

Missoula was still sprinkled with the rambling and rotting mansions left over from the lumber baron days, and Sam's room was under the eaves of one of these surviving monsters. It seemed to soak in the heat through the shingles. After the first day, Sam took to spending most of his time in one of the several air-conditioned bars that fringed the campus. He came back to the room only after dark, and even then the bedroom steamed and smelled of dry rot.

Sam would open his window all the way to the top and sit on the wide sill, his stiff leg propped on the bed, smoking in the dark and feeling the breeze from the drooping trees just below. At first he tried reading, but the light attracted tiny gnats that found their way through his chest hair and even under the elastic of his shorts, so he stopped reading.

Sitting in his shorts in the dark, smoking and flicking ashes off into the dark leaves below, he listened to the play-by-play broadcast of the baseball game that drifted out of windows up and down the street, its crackle mixed with the small sounds of insects and occasional passing cars. The darkness was good to that neighborhood, for it hid the peeling paint and loose shingles of the big old houses and the seediness of their lawns.

Nobody was doing anything to repair these houses, because they were under sentence. The university had bought the land and in the fall a contractor would begin to raze the houses and cut down the rotting elms that lined the street. A new dormitory complex would take their place. In the meantime the residents droned on, bending arthritic joints to take in papers and water the browning grass and collect the last rents from the summer students. Sam shut them out, along with the other lodgers in his house, the cockroaches, the gurgling plumbing, and the urine stains on the shower walls. This shutting out was an art that he had perfected several years ago as an undergraduate, and he practised it as he sat in the window in the dark, concentrating on thinking of nothing, making his mind a blank, guarding against images and sensations until his surroundings were gone and he could sleep.

But one evening about three weeks after he had rented the room, he looked down from his window and saw a large white dog padding down the sidewalk on the other side of the street. It was an enormous German shepherd, nearly three feet at the shoulders, with a great ruff that would have made it look like a wolf if it had not been cream colored. In the twilight it was like a ghost, except for its deliberate, unhurried gait. With lowered head and flattened ears it continued around a corner and disappeared behind an untrimmed hedge.

Sam ground out his cigarette on the window sill and rubbed his stiff knee. Now with his protective blankess broken, he could hear the baby squalling downstairs, the baseball broadcast, and traffic sounds from downtown Missoula. Sam lit another cigarette and began again.

The next night he was watching for the dog. This time he saw that it came from the direction of the campus and that it accompanied a girl in blue jeans. The dog was just the same, hulking and pale, and Sam watched until it disappeared behind the same hedge. Then he turned on the light and shut the window to keep out the gnats. He was behind in his reading for the Poe seminar.

Sam had never liked Poe, not since he was eight and his mother had read him "The Telltale Heart." As far as Sam could remember, that was the only story that she had ever read to him, for his mother was a big jumpy woman, a great golfer and no reader herself. But this one time she had been between husbands and golf tournaments, and she had briefly courted Sam. "The Telltale Heart," however, had been a screaming failure, sending Sam into a state of sniveling terror for days. And his mother had thrown the book spinning into a corner, where it lay with its pages crumpled, collecting dust until Sam's grandmother rescued it on one of her tours of housekeeping duty.

It was no wonder, Sam thought in retrospect, that he had been frightened. The damned thing, beating and beating under the floorboards, was enough to scare anybody, let alone the miserable narrator and the eight-year-old boy, the two of whom had screamed in unison when Sam's mother reached the climax. Even now it was all he could do to skim through the story for the seminar. He could imagine just how the narrator had felt, burying the thing, hiding it under the floor, then hearing it throbbing away like the motorcycle that seemed to have stalled a block away, chugging fitfully. With the noise of the motorcycle came the other sounds of the night, and Sam swore and tossed away Poe for the evening.

The Poe seminar was working its way through the short stories of Poe, and the next day the instructor asked Sam what "The Fall of the House of Usher" was about. Sam, who had glanced at the story just before class, dug at the cover of the paperback with his pencil point.

"Well," he said, hating Hertz, the instructor, "the guy thinks he's buried his sister alive—"

Everyone was looking down the table at him, the brown-faced married student who lived in Sam's apartment house and the miscellaneous high school teachers and the two or three professional graduate students who called Hertz by his first name.

"Oh, sure," said Hertz, and summarized the plot, which Sam at least knew. Hertz paced along the seminar table with his head on one side like a robin's and his eyes bright. "Okay," he finished, "so what?"

The boy from Sam's mansion came to the rescue. "Usher is burying his secret desires," he said glibly. "His incestual longings for his sister, which he's unable to face up to, and tries to suppress—"

Hertz jumped on that one, and pecked at it, and one of the women disagreed. Sam, his face hot and his stiff knee itching, waited out the time until the bell rang, and fled.

He lurched down the air-conditioned hall, not trusting himself to look back, and shouldered through the plate glass doors that opened out into the brilliant sunshine and a vista of cultured Douglas firs. Blinking, Sam took two steps and stumbled over something that moved and yelped. He looked down, squinting against the glare on the cement, and met the yellow eyes of the big cream-colored German shepherd. Sam backed down the steps.

"Hey, Butler," said the boy, his neighbor, coming through the plate glass. "What'd you do, fall over Jerri's dog?"

"Whose?" said Sam warily.

The boy—Reardon was his name, Sam remembered—snapped his fingers at the dog, but she turned away and gazed at Sam with her deep yellow eyes. "Hey, girl! Where's Jerri?"

Sam waited, shifting off his stiff leg, wanting to escape but feeling as though he were caught in unfinished conversation. Reardon grinned.

"Come and have a beer," he offered. "Don't let Hertz get you down." Then, without a pause, "name's Ursula. Beauty, isn't she?"

"Oh, the dog! Ursula?"

"Right—used to belong to this kid—" They crossed the grass, detoured around a palisade of Douglas firs and a building under construction, and waited on the street corner for the traffic light to change.

"From the East, aren't you?" asked Reardon.

"New Jersey."

"Must be quite a change."

"Yes." They crossed the street, backs turned to the perpendicular mountains that closed in the northeast side of Missoula. Sam, who had flown to Missoula and had first seen the relatively harmless prairie country on the west side of town, supposed he should say something about the beautiful country. But the mountains were appalling. He had been horrified by the mountains when he first came face to face with them. Face to face was the right expression. The town and campus were spread over flat land, and suddenly the mountain was there, at right angles with the ground. Ugly mountains, too, bare and crisscrossed by horse trails and scanty shrubs that failed completely to screen occasional couples copulating behind them.

Then Sam and Reardon were across the street, and entering the bar, and there on the linoleum in front of them lay the cream-colored German shepherd. Sam backed away.

"Come on, here's Jerri," said Reardon. "What's the matter?" He sat down opposite the girl, and Sam, circling Ursula, sat down beside him. Ursula heaved herself to her feet, padded over to them with an accompaniment of toenail clicks on the linoleum, and sat down.

Sam shifted his stiff leg and looked in the other direction, at the cracking red leatherette around the bar, the sparkling technicolor scenic beer advertisements, the television set in the corner with its eternal baseball game. A pair of balding graduate students were lowering over mugs of beer in the next booth, and an old man with whiskers and logger boots was asleep in the corner under the television set. The girl opposite was watching him, and when he stole a glance over his shoulder, the dog, too, watched him with her opaque yellow eyes.

"What's with that dog?" he asked Reardon.

Reardon drank the foam from his beer. "She's sure interested in you, all right," he agreed, apparently noticing the dog's stare for the first time. "Look at her, Jerri."

"I see her," said the girl. "She likes him."

Sam set down his beer mug. His leg twinged. The dog's stare and the girl's slanted appraisal embarrassed him.

A black-haired young man in a college sweatshirt and cowboy boots came into the bar, looked around, and saw Reardon.

"O'Donnell," Reardon introduced him vaguely. "From Butte."

O'Donnell sat down by the girl and snapped his fingers at Ursula, who barely looked at him before letting her muzzle sink down to the floor. Her eyes remained fixed on Sam.

"Get your application for your antelope permit filed?" Reardon asked O'Donnell. They ordered more beers and talked about hunting while Sam stared at his mug and the dog sighed.

O'Donnell had shot a bull elk last year. He and Reardon discussed the exact gully on the exact ridge of a certain spur of mountains fifty miles from Missoula where O'Donnell had shot his elk. It had been, said O'Donnell, a hell of a job getting him back to the road.

"You hunt?" he asked Sam.

"No." What Sam had seen of the mountains was enough. They seemed to rise up forever from the barren mountains that threatened the campus to the remote ranges, pine covered to the timberline, tipped with snow in summer and gouged by the logging roads.

Reardon glanced at Sam. "Hell of a big country, all right," he agreed with Sam's thought. "I got a mountain sheep license two years ago—my God, what a great break, you know what the odds are? But I never used it. I couldn't get anybody to go in with me—you were still in the army—" O'Donnell nodded—"and it's just too damn wild back there to go alone. If you get hurt, you know—fall and break a leg, or something, you're grizzly bait. So I never used it."

Sam eyed Reardon. The boy was square shouldered, with bright, darting eyes like O'Donnell's. "Are you a good hunter?"

"Sure, hunted all my life. You never have?"

"No."

Reardon's eyes darted toward Sam's leg, but he did not comment. "Christ, if I couldn't get clear out of town once in a while, I'd go off my gourd. It's great out there, especially in winter when the deep snow's on. Clean—you know?"

Sam didn't know. "But dangerous."

"Oh, sure. You have to have some sense. Let somebody know about where you're hunting, carry some candy bars, take a partner if you're going too far back. Now, with the loggers slashing hell out of things, it's harder to get lost." Reardon stopped and drank beer soberly. "They'll ruin the whole wilderness in a few years," he went on. "Every year the pressure to open the Bob Marshall wilderness to loggers gets stronger. They'll do it yet."

"You can drive places now, it'd taken you two days to pack into a couple years ago," added O'Donnell.

"Scares the elk out. And the bears." And Reardon was off on a story about a bear that had once wandered down into Missoula and had climbed a tree in front of the Sigma Nu house, where he clung for hours while the students cut classes to stare at him. Brickbats and bee bee guns having failed to dislodge him, a policeman with a rifle finally killed him. That wouldn't happen any more, according to Reardon, for the bears were moving back into the hills.

"A grizzly?"

"Oh, God, no. A black," said Reardon, with a hasty glance at Jerri. "No grizzly'd come down into town."

"But there are more grizzlies in Montana than any other state but Alaska," said Jerri suddenly. She leaned back in her corner of the booth, watching Sam with half a smile on her narrow face, playing with her beer mug. Both Reardon and O'Donnell were abruptly silent, as the beer mug spun around and around between her thin brown fingers.'

"Back in these hills?" asked Sam.

"Some."

"What's exciting is packing in to fish," Reardon inserted hastily. "When you're hunting, at least you've got a rifle. Wait till you're carrying nothing but a spinning rod and see how you feel."

"Don't they attack people?"

That was the wrong question. O'Donnell and Reardon were off on a debate of apparent long standing, Reardon maintaining that if you used good sense and didn't go poking behind windfalls or looking for cubs, you were fairly safe. O'Donnell began to count off people he had known or known of who had used all caution and had been mauled or killed or escaped narrowly. There was the packer's wife who had run, stumbled, then played dead while a grizzly gnawed off one buttock; the hiking university students who had escaped to a tree from which they listened to the screams of an unlucky friend—"And there was always what happened in Glacier Park."

"They've attacked more people in the last year or so, all right," Reardon finally agreed. "You can't blame them, though. We keep pushin' back. Taking their territory—"

"Hell," said O'Donnell, looking absently at the brooding dog.

"Read the Lewis and Clark journals," said Jerri all at once. She looked directly at Sam, as though measuring the effect of her pedantic tone. "They had more trouble from the grizzlies than they did from Indians. The Indians themselves were scared stiff of them. *Ursus horribilus.* The Indians called them monsters."

"Maybe so, but they're making a last stand." Reardon sounded scandalized. "What are there, maybe eighty grizzlies left in this state?"

O'Donnell shrugged, eyes going from Jerri to the dog. Both young men seemed ill at ease.

"Why do you want to hunt out there?" Sam asked, baffled at their edginess. "Just the big Hemingway thing?"

Reardon laughed, but O'Donnell didn't. "You'd know if you went." Jerri half turned toward him, but he went on. "My old man worked in the copper pits, but he hunted all he could. And so do I. There aren't many of us left that can go out and hunt the way we do, just a few of us on the edge of the wilderness."

Sam stared, wondering what O'Donnell was trying to say.

"State's sprinkled with dude ranches and packer outfits. Hell, men fly in from the east coast, from the south, jet in here to hunt. It's one of the last places left."

"You're talking a lot of rot," said Jerri. "You and your damned mystique."

"Come on, Jerri," began Reardon, but O'Donnell laughed then. "I've got to meet my wife," he said, and laid down change for his beer.

Jerri watched him under sullen brows. "All right, I'm sorry," she muttered.

"Come on, Jerri," Reardon began again. "Don't be so damned touchy. He can't help it, any more than I can."

"I know," she said listlessly. Her hair had fallen over one side of her face. "See you later, when I'm not so bitchy." As she left the bar, the dog rose and gave Sam a last stare before padding after her.

"Her husband got lost in the wilderness, eighteen months ago," Reardon said at last. "They never found him, they think maybe a bear got him."

Sam sat silent. He was sitting directly under an air conditioner, and he felt as if it were forming miniature icicles of sweat up and down his arms.

"Leo raised that dog from a pup," Reardon went on, "he had two of those white pups, I remember. I'd never seen a white German shepherd before. That was—six years ago. Something happened to the other pup, but this one—Ursula—used to go everywhere with him."

"Hunting?"

"He didn't hunt, exactly. He poked around. Took some courses in zoology, guess that had something to do with it. I saw him one time, when I was elk hunting, thirty miles back from the road. He was past me before I knew he was anywhere around, just trotting along a deer trail, and Ursula about ten feet behind him."

"What happened?"

"He didn't really hunt," Reardon repeated. "You'd see him, even just a few miles from town. Looking under rocks, watching bugs or something. Then he went out for a weekend, and he never came back."

The air conditioner hummed. "Ursula went with him," Reardon went on, repeating a well-known sequence. "Leo left here with the dog on Friday. He didn't come home on Sunday. On Monday night Ursula came home alone. That's why we all thought a bear got him. Ursula would never have left him."

"Did they—look for him?"

"Oh, Jesus, they had a hell of a search. The forest service, and the sheriff's office, and private planes, and volunteers from Missoula—hell, from all over. His parents flew up from Colorado and stayed here three weeks. Nothing."

Sam shook his head, seeing the mountains, jagged teeth stained with snow and old burns and reddening juniper. He could picture, not Leo being torn by a bear, but Leo becoming nothing on the teeth of the mountains.

"That dog likes you," Reardon remarked. "You do look a little like him—"

"Seems like she's everywhere I go," Sam muttered, then stiffened, for Ursula, taking advantage of a stranger's leaving the bar, shouldered through the open door and fixed Sam with her yellow eyes. Sam choked, paid for his beer, and fled.

Sam found another bar and spent the rest of the afternoon nursing tap beers under another air conditioner. Toward evening he emerged and made his way back to the mansion, driven by a wind that had risen without warning. It scuttled dust and loose pebbles across the streets, whipped water from the lawn sprinklers, tore at loose shingles, and howled.

Sam's landlady was standing on the porch, shaking her dust mop at the wind when Sam finally got home.

"The Hellgate wind," she roared, brandishing the mop. "How do you like it?"

"I don't," Sam shouted. He looked back over his shoulder, half expecting to see the white dog. Even inside the mansion, the wind made itself heard. A tree branch shredded its leaves against a window. Sam climbed the stairs, relieved that nothing followed him, and shut his own door behind him.

The whole attic creaked, but the air was still stifling hot. Sam stripped to his shorts and sat down by the window. When he opened it, he was hit in the face by a blast of dust, so he closed it again and stood looking out across the trees and rooftops to the mouth of the Hellgate, a narrow gorge between the mountains that funneled the wind down upon the town. In the winter it could be vicious, Sam had been told. He stood nearly naked in the little room, dripping with perspiration and listening to the wind ram against the shingles. Then, when the bedroom was almost completely dark, someone rapped on the door.

Sam grabbed his pants and stepped into them, reaching for the light switch. He zipped his fly and went to the door. It swung open, and there in the darkened hall, looming larger than life, stood Ursula. She looked up at him as he stood shaking with the insane thought that she had come for him.

Then he looked past the dog and saw that Jerri, now wearing a light summer dress, stood behind her.

"Can I come in?"

"Yeah, sure," Sam muttered. He stepped back out of the way, and the dog padded into the room, followed by the girl.

Ursula looked once around the room and lay down by the window where she could watch Sam. The girl came in more slowly and stopped near the bed, looking at her hands.

"Those guys this afternoon, I don't know what you thought," she began, her voice hesitant after its earlier stridency.

Sam was embarrassed. "I don't know. I like Reardon—"

"I don't know what's the matter with me. They're both fine. When my husband was lost—" She looked up for the first time—"Mike O'Donnell spent three weeks backpacking the trails. Until he had to go to the army. That's—" Her voice dwindled again. "Hunting, hunting. It must look strange to you."

"I'm no hunter," Sam agreed. He could not understand what she was saying.

"Every time they go hunting, they ruin a little more of it. They can't see it. Oh, maybe they do. Leo did, a little. So do you, don't you?"

"Yes, in a way," he began, but Jerri went on.

"What the hell, what the hell are they going to do when it's all gone, when they can't go out? You're from the East, you see it, don't you? It must," and she was listless again, "be wonderful to come from outside. They're all alike here."

The dog brooded, and Sam looked from her to the girl. "What makes her watch me?" he asked.

Jerri broke away from her thoughts, startled. "I don't know—she does, doesn't she? You do," she added, "look a little like Leo. Mike thinks so."

The dog sighed and got ponderously to her feet.

"I suppose I'd better go," Jerri said, and the dog came and stood beside her. They left together, leaving the door open behind them, and Sam could hear Ursula's toenails scratching on the stairs all the way to the bottom. When the door at the foot of the hall slammed, he turned off the light and sat down on the bed in the dark.

The next morning the wind was gone. Sam was cautious on the stairs and on the way to the campus, but he saw no white dog all that day or the next. Relieved, he began again on his wall of protection. On the third day after Jerri's visit, as he was walking back to the mansion after his Poe seminar, a car pulled over and stopped.

Sam paused. Jerri was behind the wheel, and the tips of Ursula's ears rose over the back of the seat. Jerri's hair was brushed smooth, and she smiled, showing even teeth.

"Let me give you a lift," she offered.

"It's not very far."

"Doesn't matter." She smiled again, leaning forward against the open window.

Sam shrugged and went around to the door on the passenger side. Ursula looked up at him from the back seat. Sam kept his back turned to her, but the hair on the back of his neck prickled.

"I don't live this way—"

"I know. Come for a ride with me?" She looked away from the street to smile at him. They passed an intersection, and someone's brakes squealed. Sam sank into his seat.

They turned up the highway that led through the Hellgate, going much too fast, and Sam leaned against the window to look up the sheer and pine-bristling cliffs that rose perpendicularly from the road.

"Where are we going?"

"Just up the road a little way." They turned sharply, brakes protesting, on a rough-graded dirt road that wound uphill through a grove of second-growth poplar and straggling pine. Then the poplars faded out, and Sam had a clear view of miles upon miles of mountains, stretching peak upon peak into bluer and bluer distance. A meadow opened on the lower side of the road, rank with lupine and swamp grass. The road grew narrower, and ended against a row of boulders.

"Just a pack trail from here," Jerri explained. She turned off the ignition and Sam slumped against the seat. His stomach churned from the ride. A bird whistled.

Jerri got out of the car and came around to Sam's open window. "We can't drive any farther," she repeated.

"I don't want to walk anywhere." He felt another wave of nausea.

Jerri let Ursula out of the back seat. The dog stretched, then trotted over to the boulders that barred the road. She stopped and looked back over her shoulder, waiting.

The scent of pines and grass blew through the open windows of the car, but Sam felt suffocated. He did not want to get out of the car. Its upholstered frame suddenly seemed comforting. But Jerri stood waiting, and he felt foolish crouching in the car. He opened the door and got out gingerly, testing the ground with his foot before he trusted his weight on it. The layers of rotted pine needles shifted under him, and his knees felt weak after his rocketing ride. Ursula waited, head raised, body motionless.

Jerri took his hand. She had smooth, narrow, brown fingers, and she drew him toward the boulders where Ursula waited. Sam stumbled after her self-consciously. Ursula, seeing that they were coming, trotted between the boulders and down the trail fifty feet, where she stopped again and looked back.

Jerri smiled at him. The collar of her shirt stood away from her body, exposing a line of smooth tanned flesh. "Reardon and Mike O'Donnell and all the others, they're all alike. Such great hunters, telling about their first elk or their first deer, and remembering every twig they ever snapped or every grouse they ever gutted—" She had led him past the boulders and around a bristling clump of juniper. Sam, looking back, could no longer see the car. Jerri gazed up at him.

"You're not like that, are you?"

"No." That, for God's sake, was the truth. Except for recent conversations with Reardon and O'Donnell, Sam's notion of hunting was gleaned from books he had had to read in some course in literature, about boys shooting their first deer and smearing their cheeks with blood, or old men who somehow rejuvenated themselves on similar trips. The air around him was still deep with pine and snow from higher in the mountains, but Sam's nausea rose, sour in his throat. Jerri was very close to him.

"I knew you were different. You don't need to spoil anything, do you? The way they start out, with guns to protect themselves, having to kill something out there to keep themselves together, it's frightening. But you don't need that, do you?"

Sam stopped, looking from the girl to the dog that stood stolidly waiting. "I?" he managed. The nausea was worse. Beside him, Jerri's eyes were immense, and as Sam took a step backward she reached out to hold him.

"Don't you think I'm attractive?" she whispered.

Sam, shaking, swallowed back the flush of bile. Jerri held his hand, and before he could draw back she had taken the step that lay between them and had driven one brown hand under his belt, under the band of his shorts and down toward his groin.

Sam jerked back, retching. He stumbled a few feet off the trail and vomited into the lupine.

"For God's sake," he begged after a moment, "I'm sick, won't you take me back to town?"

Jerri had waited on the trail, making no move to help him. Now she shrugged and nodded. Ursula turned slowly back and sniffed at the lupine before trotting off toward the car. Sam, limp, followed her.

Jerri drove slowly and carefully all the way back to town and stopped under a decayed elm in front of Sam's mansion.

"Sam," she said then, and her voice quavered, but Sam dragged himself out of the car and across the porch without looking back. He climbed the stairs, one foot at a time, and closed his door behind him. There in the heat, in the yellow light from the window, he threw himself down on his bed. A few minutes later he got up and rinsed his mouth, then lay down again, hugging his knees and feeling hot tears behind his eyelids. His heart pounded, and he did not get up again until the room was wholly dark.

He skipped several days of classes, and when he came out of his room again, he kept his head down and ignored his neighbors. Reardon looked curiously at him when they passed on the stairs, but said nothing. When the summer term ended, Sam bought an airline ticket back to New Jersey. The only bad moment was when he looked from the airplane window down upon the jaws of the Hellgate and the jagged teeth of the mountains.

Paths Unto the Dead

Successive ice ages had shaped the land, as though a careless sweep of clawed fingers had gouged the still-malleable plains into plateau and valley. Thus cruelly torn, the land became harsher. The hills lay bare under the sweep of the galaxy, waiting from the beginning of time until the end. These years, wheatfields rolled their seasonal gold across the prairie, a momentary phenomenon that would soon be gone. Already the fine dust of the hot season filtered over fields, fences, and the fragile tracks of men.

The river bottom offered some protection. Here, at the foot of a narrow road through the bluffs, willows grew along the water. The milk cow and her heifer had found shade at the foot of their pasture, where they waited, switching flies and watching the house for signs of milking time. Nearer the buildings the hens clucked their concerns of the moment from their dust nests under the chokecherries.

The white frame house and its little patch of lawn were overhung by a seventy-year-old maple. The tree was one of several saplings that had been brought hundreds of miles by buggy; only this one had survived the first killing winter, but now it spread patterned green shade over the porch where the women sat and had sprouts of its own around the base. Like the women who sat in its shade and rocked, the tree had settled into a bitter world for the course of its span.

Two of the women on the porch were white-haired. They resembled each other, though in fact they were related only by marriage. Both were physically strong women; they both had light-blue eyes—childlike eyes, the young woman thought—and wore starched homemade dresses. Years of chores in garden and barnyard had left their arms and faces as brown and seamed as walnuts.

The thinner of the two old women jumped to her feet with surprising ease and shaded her gaze with her hand.

"That cat's got kittens hidden somewhere. Look at her, there she goes to the barn with another mouse."

The other old woman, her sister-in-law, continued to rock. "I expect the place can hold another batch of kittens, Dorothy."

"They'll grow up wild and bother the hens."

"Jeff's little girls will tame them when they come to visit."

"They'll be too much for the little girls. They'll be wild and spry by the time the girls get here," Dorothy countered, but her arguments had the lack of conviction of a spinster in the presence of a woman who has been married.

"Jeff's little girls have grown. I hardly knew little Peggy when I saw her at the funeral." The rocking chair's gentle motion continued. "So many of Lavinia's friends there, and so many flowers."

"It was the first funeral I ever went to where they didn't have the obituary read," objected Dorothy. "That surprised me. I wonder whose idea that was."

The young woman, Jean, who sat on the porch steps, was familiar enough with her great-aunts' patterns of response that she could have predicted every word, though it had been three years since she had last listened to them. The limitations of their conversation, the sunbaked barnyard, and the dark little house with its oilcloth and spotty floors depressed her as much as the desultory talk of her grandmother's funeral, only a week past. The visit with the two old ladies was paid out of duty and the memory of past affection; but already she toyed with ways to escape ahead of time. "Jean begins to look like Lavinia, doesn't she?" her Aunt Emily observed unexpectedly. Her rocking chair continued its unhurried rhythm.

Aunt Dorothy turned from her observation of the gray barncat's doings and gave Jean a sharp, considering look.

"I never thought of it before, Emily."

Emily laid her knitting in her lap and rocked on. Her blue eyes were faraway. "I was thinking about Lavinia and how she looked at the time she taught at the Bally-Dome. She was about the age Jean is now."Dorothy looked critically at her great-niece. "The way you girls wear your hair now, all skinned back, and those steel-rimmed glasses! You'd be right in style for my day, Jean."

Jean smiled politely and tucked a wisp of brown hair behind her ear, but inwardly she felt familiar resentment rising that anyone could think that she, Jean, was what these old women once had been. Her own supple brown hands lay loosely in the lap of her short cotton dress; her aunts' hands, always filled with knitting or sewing or food or tools, were gnarled, stiffened with too much heavy work and scarred by work that was too dangerous. Aunt Emily had a deep mark on her wrist that Jean knew was a rope burn, and both old women could display nicks and troughs on their fingers that had been left by knives, mowing-machine teeth, or barbed wire. Any prettiness that they might have had, they had used up right away, Jean thought with resentment. It was as though prettiness were something to be left behind as soon as possible; and she looked with protectiveness at her own smooth fingers.

Emily resumed her knitting. "I always thought Lavinia was the prettiest of Edward's sisters."

"Pretty is as pretty does," said Dorothy sharply, but she was ready to yield to the pleasure of reminiscence. "I was ten years old when you married Edward and came here to live. We all had new dresses for the wedding, and all the neighbors came—I remember the buggies coming across the fords. Alice was fourteen then and Lavinia was eighteen."

And now there were only Emily and Dorothy, Jean supplied to herself. Alice dead in young womanhood, Edward in middle age. And Lavinia, her grandmother, buried last week. And yet the voices of the two old women were as undisturbed and light, dropping off into the sunlight as inconsequentially, as the clicks of the knitting needles or the unruffled sounds of the hens in the heat of the day.

"Doesn't it bother you to talk about them?" she demanded without thinking, and bit her lip the next moment; but the old ladies exchanged indulgent looks over her head.

"Now, Jean, what will be, will be," said Emily gently, and Dorothy nodded her small white head from her seat on the porch railing. Jean again felt the resentment rise, but her aunts' voices pattered on.

"Hard to believe Lavinia was ever as skinny as Jean."

"She wasn't," Dorothy objected. "None of us ran to skin and bones the way the girls do today. We all had flesh."

Aunt Emily knitted on decisively. "Dorothy, you don't remember. Lavinia had an elegant slim figure as a young woman. It was after she was married and the babies came, and things were so hard out there on the homestead that she went to flesh."

Dorothy looked mulish. Then she slid off her perch on the porch railing and crossed to the door with her surprisingly easy steps. "I'll just get Mama's album."

Aunt Emily knitted on, but her mouth twitched. It was the closest she ever came to a smile. "My mother-in-law —that was your great-grandmother, Jean—used to say that Dorothy could never sit still long enough to get married."

Dorothy came back through the screen door, carrying the large plush-covered album. She looked suspiciously at her sister-in-law. "Guess I can sit still. Doesn't mean I wanted to get married, though."

Jean knew the album from childhood. The dusty blue plush under her fingertips recalled sticky afternoons on Aunt Emily's porch with her cousins, eating fried chicken and giggling over the clothes and stiff postures of their elders, while the originals of many of the photographs drowsed in the parlor after their Sunday dinner. Some of the faces in the album she could still name, not because she could associate these youthful lines and planes with the people she had known (in almost every case the known face seemed to Jean to be so changed as to be completely unconnected with the early likeness), but from summer afternoons of clamoring, "Who's that, Aunt Emily? Who's that in the buggy? On the fence?" It was inconceivable, for example, that her own grandmother, whom Jean had known as a broad, silent old woman with painfully misshapen feet and joints, could ever have been the startled child whose high woolen collar seemed to be throttling her. Or that her grandfather, that mysterious suspendered mountain wheezing in his chair, had a counterpart in the narrow-chinned youth peering slyly at the camera from beneath his greased wings of hair.

To the child, there had simply been no connection between the fading likenesses and the known flesh; that Aunt Emily always replied to the constantly reiterated "Who's that?" with "That's your Aunt Dorothy when she started school in town," or "That's my father with his buggy horse, and the boy holding the halter went away to Cuba and was killed," or "That's your grandfather when he first filed on the homestead," was only a game in which Aunt Emily always managed to parry the child's unbelieving questions with an outlandish but unassailable answer.

The young woman, however, began to see remembered likenesses as her aunts turned the crumbling black pages. Here a tilt of a head, there a scowl. Recognizing these faces of the dead, somehow caught here for a little while in fading photographs pasted to album leaves that after seventy years were beginning to decompose, with names and histories remembered by the two old women (how long before the names went to the grave and the photographs became dust?) made her uneasy, and she looked off across the sunbaked barnyard with distaste.

Dorothy, who had forgotten her purpose in fetching the album, called Jean's attention to a posed studio portrait of four small children.

"Do you know which is your father?"

"The second one," Jean answered automatically. *Who's that, Aunt Emily?* But looking more carefully at the six-year-old boy in the constricting collar, she could see the line of eyebrows and nose, the set of the eyes, that would become the besieged outlook of the man.

Emily looked over from her rocker. "That picture was taken in March, just before they moved out to the homestead."

"The spring of the diphtheria epidemic."

"And Jeff was born that summer."

After the little girls died of diphtheria, Jean added to

herself. The children stared out at the photographer, pale above their unnaturally confining clothing.

"How did she stand it?" she cried. "She had eight children and lost five. Two of diphtheria, two of influenza, one drowned. Living out there on the homestead for days and days without seeing anybody, and there isn't even a tree in sight. Carrying all her water a quarter of a mile, and Grandfather never ever talked, to her or anybody else—"

The old ladies looked at each other again, and Emily knitted carefully to the end of her row. "Things come to us, and we meet them. Your grandmother did her duty, same as we all did." She seemed to recognize that her words were untranslatable to her great-niece and laid down her needles. She sat for a moment, turning her stiffened hands palm upward, and Jean remembered that Emily had also lost a child in the diphtheria epidemic.

"Things pass," said Emily at last.

Jean looked away. The sun beat on the little board walk, wilting the grass and Aunt Dorothy's row of sweet peas. Heat shimmered over the bare road and the dusty chokecherries beyond it. One chicken chased another with a ruffling of white feathers through the weeds on the other side of the fence, and the gray cat emerged from the barn, looking carefully in all directions before disappearing into the weeds on her own business. The dusty little circle seemed all at once not merely tedious, but suffocating. Of course, things passed. Their lives had passed with no more disturbance and less comfort than the lives of the chickens that Aunt Dorothy fed and that Aunt Emily would stew for Sunday dinner, one by one, or the existence of the cautious barncat, who would watch for field mice until a hawk sighted her and plummeted successfully.

Jean took a deep breath. Her own life would pass, the days would dawn and fade, but at leats she had *had* something. She plucked at the hem of her expensive cotton dress, noting again the flexibility of her tapering brown fingers, the glint of the sun on her handcrafted bracelet. Unlike her grandmother and her great-aunts, she had her job and her clothes, her records and books and her glimpses of what she still thought of as the "outside world," if not at first hand, at least through foreign films.

She had lived in the city and visited coffee houses and discotheques, and she had slept with three men. All this Jean offered up as a shield between herself and the smothering energy of the sun. At least she had had experiences.

Aunt Dorothy looked from her sister-in-law's face to her niece and turned a leaf in the album. "That's Jesse MacGregor," she said. "He came over here from Scotland and herded sheep for my father. Your great-grandfather's sheepherder, Jean."

Jean had seen the picture before, but she looked obediently, squinting as sunlight fell over the page. The man leading a horse in the picture wore the drab clothing and heavy moustache that the child remembered. To the child, the unfamiliar face had been no-age, a face out of the undifferentiated limbo of grownupness. The young woman saw, as if through an overlay of memory, that Jesse MacGregor had an energetic cock of his head and high spirit in his face that turned, not toward the horse he led, but toward the photographer. Jesse MacGregor had been a young man on the day someone with a complicated camera had troubled to go through the ritual of recording the face of a hired sheepherder from Scotland.

"Lavinia took that picture," Emily said. "She bought the camera in the late fall, with the first of her school money from the Bally-Dome."

Dorothy looked sharply at her sister-in-law. "Jesse MacGregor was an awful man for the drink. Papa used to say that Jesse was a dependable man until he had the first wee drink. And then nothing could keep him until he'd finished his spree."

Emily pursed her lips. "Yes, he drank."

"Why, Emily! No one ever liked to speak in front of us girls, but I can remember as clear as yesterday, Jesse riding in after dark and singing out by the water tank, and Papa would get up from the supper table without saying anything, and go out—" Dorothy's voice dwindled. "Anyway, I don't think Lavinia ever *thought* about Jesse MacGregor—"

Emily started another row. "Jesse MacGregor was a dependable man, sober. I remember—"

Jean looked up to see that Emily had let her knitting fall

into her lap again and was looking out at the bend of the river that could be seen through the willows.

"It was after I'd married Edward. Lavinia had to file on her homestead—the place on the benchland where your father lives, Jean. It was a thirty-mile ride to the county seat, too far for her to go alone, and the men were gone, Edward and his father—but Lavinia had to get in to the courthouse, and she was getting ready for the ride, and her mother was nearly beside herself. And then Jesse rode in from the sheep camp that morning. It was time for his spree.

"So Jesse said he'd ride in to town with Lavinia, and then her mother *was* wild. But Lavinia said nonsense, she had to go to town, and if Jesse MacGregor rode one way with her, she might be able to find someone who'd ride back with her. Jesse caught a fresh horse and they started out.

"Mother worried all afternoon, and all evening, and all the next morning. But late on the second day, Lavinia and Jesse rode in. Jesse stopped at the corral, changed horses, and left again. Lavinia turned her horse out and came up to the house. We were all waiting in the kitchen."

Emily plucked at her ball of yarn with her thickened fingertips. "Lavinia said they'd ridden to town, and that she had filed her claim. Then she went to her aunt's house for the night, wondering what would happen in the morning. But in the morning, Jesse MacGregor was at the door with her horse, cold sober. He rode all the way home with her, saw that she was safe, and turned around and rode thirty miles back to town for his spree."

"That's what drink can do to a man," said Dorothy.

"What happened to him?" asked Jean. She had never heard the story of Jesse MacGregor or recalled anything attached to his picture but his name.

Her aunts did not answer. Dorothy turned her birdlike white head from side to side; Emily sat quietly, withdrawn into her own thoughts.

"He was shot," Emily said at last, rousing herself. "He was shot while watching your great-grandfather's sheep, and no one ever knew who did it."

"Lavinia never gave him a thought," Dorothy insisted jealously.

"No," said Emily thoughtfully, "I don't think she ever did. Certainly not from the day she met Jefferson Evers. But it was right after that—"

"Now, Emily, you've got no business to think he did it deliberately, especially after all these years."

"Did what?" demanded Jean. "Who? My grandfather?"

"No, no," said Emily. "Jesse MacGregor. He went on a spree the day Lavinia got her engagement ring, and when he sobered up, he went up in the hills to the sheep. When they found his body, he was fifteen miles north, clear over on the Blackwell range."

"Now, Emily—"

"He knew that country well," Emily went on, as if Dorothy had not spoken. "And he knew how touchy things were getting about grazing rights. None of the men liked to discuss it in front of us, but it was rumored that the Blackwells had threatened to have any man shot who tried to steal grass."

Dorothy opened her mouth, but Emily went on, her words falling as lightly, her voice as inconsequential, as when she had talked of Lavinia's funeral or the barncat's kittens. "Jesse knew what would happen from the minute he turned those sheep north, and all the days it would have taken to drive them into strange grazing land."

Jean looked down at the picture. Jesse MacGregor's face had faded after sixty years, but the outlines of his body still expressed vigorous life.

"He was quite good-looking, wasn't he?" she asked.

"He was considered a very handsome man," Aunt Dorothy answered, crimping her mouth. "But Lavinia never looked at another man after she met Jefferson Evers."

Rays of sunlight fell through the maple leaves and whitened the picture of Jesse MacGregor, but Jean could see the lines of the young man's shouldders, the angle of his hat, with her eyes shut. She wished suddenly that she could not.

"Did Grandma know—how he felt?" she asked, uncomfortable with a vocabulary that she knew had far different connotations for her aunts.

Emily sighed. "I suppose she must have. We didn't talk of such things."

"She couldn't have married him," put in Dorothy. "All he had were the clothes he wore. And his sprees—"

"He was always a man who liked being alive," said Emily.

It was late afternoon, and Jean could leave now, get away from the scent of mildew and dust and the infirmities of old women. Tomorrow she would take the plane back home, to her own apartment and her own concerns, her own life that she protected so carefully from the decay that had found her grandmother and her aunts.

The sun was still hot, but Jean shuddered with an unfamiliar feeling of the cold. She would take back with her the story of her grandmother and Jesse MacGregor, and how Jesse MacGregor, a man who liked being alive, had deliberately turned his sheep north to unfriendly grazing land on the day her grandmother had become engaged to another man. Jean stood up and brushed off her skirt. The story of Jesse MacGregor seemed to her the first sign of the decay she feared.

"Lavinia never *thought* of Jesse MacGregor," Dorothy crooned. Jean looked up at the new note in her aunt's voice, but Dorothy was looking at Emily.

Emily rocked once, twice. The ball of yarn rolled out of her lap. "It was a long time ago," she said.

"Lavinia never thought—"

"No, no." Emily's knitting lay abandoned, a stitch or two pulled out from the unwinding ball of yarn. "Never Lavinia. I was the one who thought of Jesse MacGregor."

"Emily!" warned Dorothy.

But Jean ran the step or two down the path and picked up the escaping ball of yarn. The story of Jesse MacGregor had unwound further already than she had ever wanted to hear.

Slightly Broken

It had been a hell of a morning. A Canadian front had blown fitful, on-again off-again rain into northern Montana. Gusts of wind hurtled raindrops like handfuls of rattling peas against Rita's office window to splinter and crawl in dirty streaks to the sill. Rita crouched beside the telephone that might ring any minute but so far had been silent—another hour and she could go home, she could figure the weather was bad and he wouldn't be calling—and yawned hugely in spite of the apprehension that had gnawed away at her all morning.

She got up and refilled her coffee cup from the office urn. The urn was nearly full; no pilots had come along this morning to bum coffee off her, waste time, and kid her about how much weight she hadn't lost. Nobody would be flying in this weather. Mike wasn't going to call her, and pretty soon she could get away with going home and forgetting about him. As she turned back to the foggy window she could see the rain dripping in puddles off the wingtips of the small planes tied down in a line opposite the one-story administration building. South of the airport the cloud ceiling was settling over the gray line of buttes.

Beaver McAllister wandered across the hall from the Weather Bureau office, his dirty coffee mug in his hand. "Sure the hell quiet around here this morning," he complained. "You got any coffee left?"

Rita said nothing. Beaver turned the handle and let the thick coffee dribble into his mug, as she had known he would. He tasted it and recoiled. "Jesus Christ but this stuff's foul!"

"Go make some you like better."

Beaver shrugged; her bad temper wasn't worth his notice. Instead of going back to work he leaned on her office door and drank his coffee, staring out across the taxiways to midfield where the windsock hung, too wet to twitch, over a scattered congregation of waterlogged hay bales. Rita sat down at her desk with her back to him, disliking the freckles on his domed forehead and the slightly protruding teeth that made him look opinionated even before he started to talk.

"Did Mike leave this morning?" asked Beaver, offhand.

"Yeah—" the knowledge of what Beaver really wanted to know crossed her mind like a grate, and she rattled off the defensive words. "Yeah, he flew down to Great Falls before it started to rain this morning, he was figuring on leaving the new plane there to have the radios installed, and then he was going to call me and have me fly down in the other Skyhawk to pick him up—but now the weather's turned bad, so hard to tell what he's gonna do—" behind her back, Beaver shifted his feet; he knew damn well what Mike was doing— "so if he don't call in another twenty minutes, I'm gonna close the office and go home."

"Another front's moving in," said Beaver. "It should start to clear this afternoon."

"Good, because I ain't leaving the ground until it does."

In the silence Rita could hear the lash of fresh rain across the window and the breathy noise Beaver made when he drank his coffee. Without turning around she could see his lip curled back from the hot rim as he sucked coffee through his big horse teeth. She knew them all too well, the boys at the Weather Bureau and the Frontier Airlines agent and the pilots that hung around and shot the shit with Mike.

"I never did understand," said Beaver, "if it scares you so bad, why you wanted to learn to fly in the first place."

"Who said I got a choice?" But at the unbidden memory of Mike yelling at her from the right seat during those first flying lessons, the pang in her stomach was as sharp as if something were trying to get out. She scratched through her purse for a quarter and went to drop it in the candy machine. Her own eyes, trapped in rings of black mascara, looked out of the mirror as she punched the button for a caramel nutroll. Beaver stirred behind her, watching her; and Rita sensed his thoughts. *She could fix herself up if she wanted to. Take off twenty pounds, do her hair. She could if she wanted to, so it's her own fault if Mike plays around someplace else.*

But what he said was, "I don't see what you got to be scared of."

"I just am. I hate that goddamn plane."

"It's all in your head," said Beaver smugly.

Rita ripped back the paper from her nutroll and tore off a bite between her teeth. The syrup deadened her tongue. "Listen! Mike, he flies that plane like he was half machine himself. He don't think what to do next, he just keeps his goddamn machine running and comes down to tell how he had to go to seventeen thousand to get over the cloud ceiling or how much ice he picked up—you ever listened to him?"

"Hell, Rita, with Mike trying to keep the business running on the side, it'd be real handy for him if you'd jar loose and take your check ride. Finish your license, why don't you?"

"Real handy for him, all right," Rita muttered. "Sometimes I think he hopes I'll smear into a hill."

"And that fear, it's all in your head," repeated Beaver, proud as if it were a new piece he'd learned.

"You're goddamn right it's all in my head! I ain't no half-machine! If something goes wrong up there, I ain't got no machine in me to take over and do the right thing. All I got is what's in my head, and I got a feeling that ain't enough!"

"You women always like to let on you can do anything —" began Beaver with a smirk, but just then the telephone rang so stridently that he jumped and slopped coffee over the rim of his cup.

Rita snatched the receiver off the cradle. She knew who it was.

"Mike's Flying Service!"

Mike's voice rasped through the weather static on the long-distance line from Great Falls. "Where the hell you been?"

Rita found herself in the weary rut of defence. "What do you mean? I've been waiting here all lousy morning, watching it rain and wondering if you made it. Where the hell *you* been?"

Mike paid no attention. "Just get your ass down here and pick me up. I'll be at Lynch's Air Service."

Another skiff of rain smacked against the window. Rita looked over her shoulder and saw that a light wind was needling the rain, riling the puddles on the taxiway to a purplish haze. "But the weather's bad!" she wailed.

"The sun's shining down here."

"I don't care what it's doing in Great Falls, it's been raining here all morning and now the wind's picking up—"

"Shit," said Mike heavily between his teeth. "I just called the flight service station here, and you got your thousand feet if you get your ass out of the sling and take off right now, not an hour from now—"

"But Beaver says another front's coming!"

"Is Beaver there? Let me talk to him."

Rita handed over the receiver to Beaver, who took it with a grin, and retreated into a corner. The caramel had oozed into her lower molars and made them throb. What she could see of the cloud ceiling from the window was gray and dense, a vast blanket closing off the northern plains from the rest of the universe. But the tops of the buttes to the south were still clearly visible. She had her thousand feet of visibility, all right, she thought reluctantly.

"—yeah, another front'll move in and push all this crap on through here by late afternoon. Oh, the wind might pick up a little more, but nothing that should give her trouble if she takes off now," said Beaver. He sucked at his teeth, examining a thumbnail.

"It's rotten weather," Rita muttered, backing into her corner. "Nobody's flying today."

"All righty," Beaver said into the phone. He hung up and turned, grinning. "Mike says he'll be looking for you at Lynch's in about an hour."

Rita glared at him, hating his blank grin and his freckled

scalp. He'd just as soon she crashed, she thought. Like to see her get hurt.

"Don't mean to tell you what you better do, but the longer you wait, the nastier it's gonna be."

Rita snatched her jacket from the hook behind the door where Mike kept extra oil and charts and junk. She fumbled with the zipper, finally hooked it and jerked it to her chin. Her purse was in her desk drawer. She slung the strap over her shoulder, every motion seeming as difficult and separately defined as steps taken through water. The office had never seemed so warm and familiar.

"Remember, he's gotta get back for the three-to-eleven shift tonight," Beaver shot after her. "He has to support you and those kids of yours some way."

Rita slammed the door on him.

After her warm office, leaving the administration building and walking into the cold, sharp rain was as bad a jolt as hearing Mike's voice chopping off instructions at her. Rita tramped through puddles with her hands clenched in her pockets and her chin ducked into her collar until she reached the steel hangar that Mike had borrowed more money to erect. Then she stopped and looked back over the flat expanse of empty gray runways, feeling about as big as one of the gophers that in good weather sat on their haunches in the alfalfa to watch the shadows of the planes.

Nobody else was in sight. The gas pumps were locked and abandoned on their island fifty yards away across the paving. Even the spray planes were tied down, and the three or four trailers that were summer offices for the spray pilots had their doors closed and their windows fogged with rain. The only sign of life was a truck on the Great Falls highway south of the airport, dwarfed by distance. She could not even hear the diesel engine.

Hell, she might as well do it.

Rita leaned on the heavy transverse door. It moved reluctantly on its wet tracks, and there, its wheels on planks laid across the dirt floor, was the blue and white Skyhawk.

She walked around the wing and braced herself against the strut. It always seemed like she'd never get the damn plane moving out of the hangar until she'd strained herself out of her skin. Once it started rolling, it moved easily and she had to watch that the nose wheel stayed straight and took the plane through the door without veering left or right and damaging a wingtip against the hangar. This time the Skyhawk rolled left at the last minute. Rita caught at the strut to steady it and felt a fingernail split straight across.

Rita walked all around the little plane as she had been shown, checking the fuel caps and tires and the oil gauge. Then she took the big step up, her tight Levi's protesting against her thighs, and climbed into the left seat. She turned the door handle to the locked position and fastened her seat belt. Then she looked at her hand. It was chapped and red, the nails bloodless from the chill of the rain, and the middle fingernail had split to the quick. She began to cry.

When she stopped crying, it was because nothing had happened and she was still sitting alone behind the hangar, crammed into the chilly metal cabin of the Skyhawk. She knew what she looked like. The rain and wind had straggled through the hair she had carefully back-combed that morning, and she knew her make-up would be blotched from her tears. Always supposing she got the Skyhawk to Great Falls in one piece, she'd be a sight walking into Lynch's where Mike would be drinking coffee and wisecracking with the boys. *"Here she comes—Miss America!"* he'd barked once to a snickering circle of spray pilots when Rita had staggered in from gassing up a plane in a thirty-mile wind, her hair standing on end and her jacket reeking of gasoline fumes.

"The son of a bitch wants a beautiful wife, he might start by hiring a line boy," Rita now said out loud as her hands moved over the instrument panel in the automatic routine Mike had pounded into her. *Do it till it's second nature. You shouldn't have to think about it. You might not have time to think.* But surely she could make herself look better if she tried. Remember how she'd teased and sprayed her hair when she worked at the Hideaway, taken more trouble with her make-up. If only she could lose a few pounds.

Rita slid her seat all the way forward until her legs could reach the rudder pedals. The propeller caught, fluttered, and became a blur. Rita eased in the throttle, and the little plane moved out from behind the hangar, responding perfectly to her hand on the power and her feet on the disc brakes.

Of course, a barmaid was supposed to look pretty. There had been plenty of times when some lush was telling her what a bitch his old lady was, when Georgie's hand was in her pants behind the bar and she still didn't dare spill the drink she was mixing, that she'd had to grit her teeth to smile and remember the drunk was always right. She'd smiled and smiled, grinding her teeth all the time and reminding herself that if the lush came across with an extra fifty cents, it would pay an hour's time to the babysitter home with the two little girls. When Mike first started hanging around the Hideaway at closing time, he'd looked pretty good to her.

Big change. Now there were four kids at home instead of two, and instead of slopping drinks across the bar to drunks, she was playing line girl and gassing and taxiing airplanes and trying to learn how to keep Mike's books. And she was pretty sure which barmaid downtown thought the brakeman getting off shift at eleven o'clock looked pretty good.

Now Rita stepped hard on the right brake and brought the Skyhawk sharply around into the wind for the run-up. Her eyes checked off the routine. Oil gauge, gas gauge. Rev it up to 1700 rpms, check the carb heat, right and left mags. The little plane quivered with the power of the engine until she eased back on the throttle. Rita could remember when she had found even that roar scary.

She reached for the radio mike on its bracket.

"Havre unicom. Cessna six-eight-zero, ready for take-off on two-five."

Nobody answered. The unicom wasn't attended half the time, especially on a day like today when airport traffic was practically shut down. Nevertheless Rita swung the little plane around to clear the area as she had been taught, peering as far east as she could for any sign of incoming traffic, but the dripping gray sky was empty.

She hung the mike on its bracket, increased the throttle, and taxied out on the big runway.

"Shove the throttle all the way in, not too hard," Mike had told her. "Come back with the controls until you've cleared the ground. Then level out until your airspeed builds up to ninety. That way you lift her off gentle and you don't run a chance of a stall during take-off. Coax her along, goddamnit, like she was part of you."

Water cascaded over the windshield as the plane roared through the puddles on the runway. Rita leaned forward over the controls, her whole body a knot of concentration on the moment when she would perceive through her hands or the seat of her pants or the soles of her feet that the plane wanted to lift off. The next moment the sheets of water fell away and she was airborne.

The runway fell away behind her as she gained altitude. Rita realized from the ache in her ribs that she had been holding her breath. She expelled air and flexed the hand that had been locked, white-knuckled, on the controls. The needle on the altimeter flicked past three thousand feet and she banked and angled out of the airport pattern.

She could fly the plane all right, hold the altitude constant, and make the wind corrections to make her S-turns and rectangular courses come out the way they were supposed to, and probably she could pass her check ride and get her private pilot's license any time she worked up the nerve to go down to Great Falls and sign up for it. What scared the shit out of her was something not Mike nor Beaver nor any of the men could understand, because the very thing they thought ought to reassure her, the knowledge that the airplane would respond to her hands and feet and follow her bidding while she was all by herself up there, was what she baulked at the worst. There was something as unnatural as hell about her being in control, and the knowledge that she could do it only intensified the conviction that she was bringing about her own doom and maybe somebody else's.

She dreamed about it more and more. In the dream she might be flying routine turns about a point, five thousand feet in the blue and banking sharply on the downwind curve, when an unfocused miscalculation of hers that Mike would have known instinctively how to correct or avoid in the first place would send the Skyhawk first into a skid and then a spin, out of control and screaming earthward out of the empty sky while Rita fought her way out of the bed covers, trying to wake up enough to remember whether Mike was in bed beside her or working graveyard shift out of the yards or catting around someplace. Or she would be sitting at her desk in the middle of the afternoon, trying to work out whether Mike had made or lost money on his last charter to Minneapolis and watching the spray planes come back in for the day, when she would be gripped by a terrible fantasy of being at the controls of a small plane, flying at a hundred and twenty miles an hour into empty sky when out of nowhere a larger plane would materialize in her flight path, too close for her to avoid a head-on collision by some maneuver Mike would have pulled off without thinking. The fantasy was vivid enough to bring her trembling out of her chair and get her some funny looks from whichever pilots happened to be lazing around her office and drinking her coffee that day.

Now Rita trimmed the Skyhawk for level flight. At about a thousand feet above the ground, she could easily keep Highway 87, which angled southwest between Havre and Great Falls, in sight.

"Don't you fly a heading?" one of the men had asked her, scandalized.

"I just head whichever way I'm flying," she had wisecracked back, although of course Mike had taught her how to plot a course and work out where she was by the computer, making allowances for winddrift and all the rest.

"What if you run into bad weather?"

"I don't figure on it. If it looks like there's a drop of rain between here and where I'm going, I don't leave the ground."

Now here she was, hanging between sky and earth, while another gust of wind slapped rain across her windshield and made the plane buck like a wild thing with a mind of its own. Just a little turbulence, Rita told herself, though her grip on the controls was white-knuckled again. She leveled the wings and breathed out. One thing, she had to get the fantasies out of her mind until she landed in Great Falls.

She thought every pilot on the highline at one time or another must have watched Mike give her a flying lesson. It made a good show, Mike turning red and bellowing while Rita cried and tried to remember which way to turn the ailerons while she was taxiing into the wind. Nobody could figure out why Mike was so dead set on teaching Rita to fly. Know-it-all Beaver pointed out how handy a flying wife would be to a fellow working twenty hours a day to hold down a regular job with the railroad and establish a flying service on the side, but even that plum hardly seemed worth Mike's expenditure of rage. For a while the wise guys had a book going on which would happen first, Mike having a stroke or Rita taking her solo flight.

Rita was thinking about Mike's rage when she noticed the ragged trails of mist off her wingtips. It was the only warning she had. One minute she could look down and see the grainfields and Highway 87 with its occasional traffic like scurrying beetles; the next minute she was engulfed in the clouds.

"God," whimpered Rita, but then she clamped her lips together because the sound of her own voice, alone in the metal cabin, sounded so unreal. She could see the interior of the cabin, instrument panel and radios and the clutter of charts in the right seat. Out the window was the cowling and the wingstrut. That was all; everything else was foggy white, and only the roar of the engine told her that she was still in flight. The plane seemed motionless.

The other sound in the cabin besides the engine was her own rapid breathing, she realized, and she told herself to stop it; but before she could force herself to begin a slow and regular pattern of air in and out, the old nightmare tore loose from its fragile reins and brought the disaster fantasy galloping toward her. The plane that materialized from nowhere was suddenly looming in her windshield, there was no way to avoid a head-on collission. Rita tried to draw her knees up under her chin and roll into a ball, but the controls were in the way and her firm seatbelt kept her in place. Her own whimpers filled the cabin.

The little Skyhawk met the phantom airplane just

vhere the giant wing sprouted from its belly. Rita, rouched down in her seat against the impact, saw red and ;old pinwheels rolling in every direction. A racket was in ıer ears. Then the Skyhawk really did give a helpless little urch. The contrast between the fantasized crash and the eal lurch brought Rita out of her crouch, and she realized hat she had squeezed her eyes so tightly shut that her orehead ached when she pried them open. The racket in ıer ears was the stall warning; the propeller had fluttered nd slowed.

You shouldn't have to think about it. You might not ıave time to think. Rita's hands were pushing the nose of he plane down to gain airspeed, increasing throttle; her eet busied themselves on the rudders. The engine creamed alive and Rita's hands automatically came back vith the controls to bring the Skyhawk out of its dive. Rita erself noted this activity with astonishment. She ob- erved that the altimeter was rising rapidly and that her ands were already moving to stabilize her rate of climb.

Rita looked at the artificial horizon. It showed that the kyhawk was flying in a fifty-degree bank. Rita blinked. he was certain she was sitting upright in level flight. She ooked around. The cabin seemed level. What she could e of the exterior of the Skyhawk seemed perfectly level. he artificial horizon showed that her angle of flight was ecoming steeper. The instrument must be defective. But it was accurate, she was risking another stall. Besides, she as gaining altitude again. Rita watched while her hands nd feet brought the plane out of its bank and trimmed it r level flight.

She was unused to flying by instruments and the auto- ıatic horizon bobbled from time to time, but as long as ıe kept an eye on it she could keep the plane under ontrol. What she couldn't do was figure out what to do ext. Think, she told herself. If Mike was telling the truth bout the sun shining in Great Falls, she ought to emerge om the clouds before too long. She pushed back her cket cuff and looked at her watch. Twelve-thirty. She ad forgotten to note her take-off time.

Calm down, she told herself. She had left Havre before oon, because Beaver was still in the office. From Havre to Great Falls was an hour in the Skyhawk. The idea of flying blindly into an air traffic area brought the fragments of the nightmare airplane twitching out of the corners of her mind. But it had been badly shattered by the head-on encounter. She remembered that she would also be flying into the radar control of the air force base at Great Falls.

If she was still headed for Great Falls.

"Oh no, oh no—" Rita heard her own voice, tinny in the enclosed space. Her compass showed a southwest heading, but after her stall and loss of equilibrium, she might be headed southwest from anywhere. She wondered if Mike would try to teach his new girl friend now to fly.

You women always like to let on you can do anything —it was a furious chorus from Mike and Beaver and all the other men she had ever known. *So try it and make a fool of yourself. We'll help you. If you try it and don't make a fool of yourself, you'll be sorry. You'll be sorry.*

The cabin exploded with sunlight. Rita blinked, her eyes burning from the strain of trying to see through the opaque white shroud of clouds. Now without warning, her vision had expanded to what seemed like infinity, for the Skyhawk had emerged above a cloud ceiling that spread beneath the tiny plane like an endless field of billowing polar snow. Above the cloud field and the speck of a plane was crystal sky and brilliant sunlight that reflected off the windshield like a thousand diamonds.

The Skyhawk bounced slightly in a draft of air, then recovered. The jiggle reminded Rita that she had flown through the phantom plane but that this sparkling blue and white eternity she was trapped in was real. She began to cry.

When she stopped crying this time, it was again because nothing had happened and she and the Skyhawk were still lost above the miles of clouds. She had taken control of the plane and the unspeakable had come to pass. She could keep flying above the cloud field until she ran out of gas or she could descend blindly through the clouds without knowing what mountain or tower protruded below her, or she could figure out something else to do.

It occurred to her that the Skyhawk carried a full set of radios. She had memorized their use and passed the FAA vritten examination a year ago. Now she stared at an ıncommunicative instrument panel, her mind a blank. The radios could tell her where she was if she could penerate them, but it was as if a steel plate had dropped beween her and everything she had ever learned, leaving ıer to scratch ineffectually at the corners.

The Skyhawk's cabin was filled with sunlight that varmed the clammy metal fittings and made Rita sweat ınder her waterproof ski jacket. She started to loosen her collar, then stopped, struck by the matter-of-fact behavior of her hand on a zipper.

Rita went on and unzipped her jacket. Then she craned ıer neck, squinting against the flood of sunlight to see as ar as she could across the cloud field below. The weather eport that morning had mentioned a slightly broken cloud ceiling over northern Montana, and Beaver had said . Canadian front would blow through by afternoon.

At last she saw what might be a break in the clouds to he northwest. She banked to her right and headed the plane toward the darker line. At ten minutes past one she ooked down through a canyon of clouds and caught a glimpse of prairie and water below her.

Rita pushed down on the controls and began to descend hrough boulders and mountains of clouds that dwarfed he Skyhawk. The little plane bucked through the increasng turbulence that struck the cloud boulders from below nd rolled them southeast. Rita hung on, all the time tryng to figure out where she was. Below her stretched the ong finger of water through cutbanks and broken hills. The Missouri River, must be. Somehow she must have drifted far to the east. But if it was the Missouri it would ead her to Great Falls. Rita changed her heading to follow he water as a flurry of rain lashed the windshield, then bbed.

In a few minutes she became uneasy. The water was eading her almost due west; also, the cutbanks seemed to e choking off the stream of water, narrowing it where it hould be growing broad. Rita peered ahead through the ain-streaked windshield and saw her river end in a cluster f coulees.

"If you follow a section line, you'll always come out on

a road," one of the men had once remarked. Rita banked sharply, flying north through the rain along a fenceline between two grainfields. Remembering the empty prairie between the Montana border and Canada to the north she almost reversed her course to fly south. But she had to make up her mind sooner or later; her gas tanks were still half full, and the worst would be getting low and having to set the Skyhawk down in a stubble field someplace.

The section line became a two-track dirt road. Rita grimly holding her north course, saw a minute tractor in a muddy field (too wet to summerfallow today) and then a cluster of farm buildings. Ahead were grain elevators foreshortened and miniaturized; a country town on a paved highway.

"I'll be go-to-hell!" she muttered, astonished. Without having the slightest idea how she had gotten there, she knew where she was. The paved road was Highway 2 running east and west along the border between Montana and Canada; those blue humps were the Sweetgrass Hills and all she had to do was turn east and follow the highway to Havre. She had never been near Great Falls.

An hour later, blear-eyed from trying to see through the rain, Rita spotted the familiar buttes and hills that landmarked the home airport. As if she had never forgotten how, she dialed a Great Falls radio frequency and heard the last hour's wind and altimeter reading.

"Havre unicom," she said into the mike. "Cessna six eight-zero on five-mile final for runway seven." Her hands sped through the prelanding procedures as she craned her neck in every direction for other traffic. Water divided in twin arcs as she set the Skyhawk down.

She taxied up to the administration building and shut down. The rain had stopped; as she pushed open the door she smelled warm air and mud and the green hay at midfield. Her legs wobbled on solid ground.

Mike shot through the main door and stopped ten feet away from her. Rita stared at him. She had entirely forgotten that she had been supposed to pick him up in Great Falls.

"How'd you get home?" she asked.

"Hitch-hiked," said Mike. Then he collected himself

'Where the goddamn hell you been? When you didn't how up, I figured you'd chickened out—called Beaver and he said you left at eleven o'clock—" Mike went on 'attling, his hands jerking.

Rita looked at her watch. A quarter to three. No wonder he was tired. She slung her jacket over her shoulder and valked around Mike to the door. The rain-washed air melled good.

"—where the hell you *been?*"

"I got lost," said Rita. As she walked into the administra-ion building with Mike fuming at her heels, she could see ieads pulling back into the Weather Bureau office and the pilots' lounge, trying to act like they were minding their own business. She walked into her own office and poured cup of coffee.

"—lost?" yelped Mike.

Rita turned around and looked at him. He was ready to oil with rage, but his eyes were baffled.

"Yeah, I got in the clouds and ended up way west of vhere I thought I was," she said. The coffee was thick and itter, but she took a second gulp. "Finally flew out of it."

Mike was studying her uneasily, at a loss what to do with is anger when she did not retreat before it. "Lucky you idn't break your fool neck," he ventured.

Rita remembered the cloud field and the brilliant, eter-al blue. "The plane flew like I wanted it to," she said. Just like you told me it would."

She looked over the rim of her coffee cup at Mike's red, affled face. "I believe I'll take my check ride this week," he said, and watched Mike swell with the anger he could o longer vent.

"You'll break your neck!" he warned, reaching one last me for the weapon that had served so long.

"As long as it's no worse," said Rita. She slid down in her hair, swinging up a leg to relax on top of her desk, and rank coffee, feeling good.

Monsters

The cries of the wild geese drifted down like the November snow to the prairie, faraway as if the flocks were abandoning the world for good. Gary Jeanmaire stopped pitching hay off the rack and tipped back his head, squinting against the hard flakes that stung his face and beaded the ruff of his parka, but the geese were far above the storm front and the lowering smoke from the pulp mills away on the slopes of the Rockies. Only the disembodied cries, wild and inarticulate, pierced the cloud cover.

Gary listened until the cries faded and he was alone again in the falling snow with the silent cattle. Then he plunged his pitchfork back into the hay, jabbing and pitching until he felt warm again and had shaken away his memory of one of the old peoples' tales—that one winter the geese would migrate for the last time.

The cattle, shaggy and dumb, had never left off plodding after the hay Gary had pitched into the fresh snow. The little heifer Babe had bought at the last cattle sale tried to get her share, but the older cows butted her and drove her away. She straggled on the fringe, trying to snatch a wisp or two. When Gary pitched her a good-sized bunch of hay over the backs of the others, they turned and drove her away from that, too. They had plenty, they just didn't want to see her get any. Cattle were bound together by the herd instinct, but they had no other sense of kind. Except for their calves. They'd fight to drive predators away from the calves. Packs of dogs or coyotes or men, whatever came prowling.

Babe was wintering forty head of cattle and Gary didn't notice any were missing from the bunch trailing the hayrack until he jumped down off the load to start the tractor and pull ahead. Then he saw the dark shape under the lone box elder tree in the corner of the feedlot that butted against Highway 2. It was too dark to see much through the falling snow, but the shape had to be that old Hereford cow, gone off by herself to have her calf. Gary glanced back over the bunch. She was gone, all right.

It seemed to him a hell of a time of year for a cow to be calving, but Babe had picked her up cheap at the sale and could turn a few dollars if he could get her and the calf through till spring. She was artificially inseminated. Those big calves from the frozen sperm of foreign bulls, Charolais and Simmental and Chianinna, were weighing maybe a hundred and twenty, hundred and thirty pounds at birth and were bringing fancy prices, but they were a bitch to calve out. Too many of those big artificial calves were coming out backwards, too many hiplocked cows in labor. It seemed to Gary to be what came of fucking around with what was natural.

He finished feeding and turned to drive his pitchfork into one of the uncut bales when he saw Babe just coming out of the shed, a bucket in each big hand. He knew Babe couldn't hear him over the roar of the tractor, but he yelled and waved anyway. As if by instinct, Babe looked up, and Gary gestured down toward the box elder tree and the cow under it. Babe looked and nodded to show he understood, then trudged on with his buckets of feed. A few minutes later Gary saw him making his way across the far end of the feedlot, bearlike in his snow-crusted mackinaw. Babe took good care of his stock; Gary gave him that much.

Gary drove the tractor out of the feedlot, closed the gate behind him, and parked the outfit in the lee side of the shed. Already the yard was buried in a sweep of white, and the roofs of Babe's shabby buildings, and all the prairie between Babe's place and the Sweetgrass Hills, which the old people said belonged to the ghosts. Gary turned up the seat of the tractor and turned off the lights, careful as always of Babe's property. Working for Babe Boniface was something he'd have said he'd never do, back five years ago when he was a senior in high school and Babe was still county sheriff. These days he'd never say there was a thing he knew he'd never do.

Hard grains of snow shook off the floor as he pulled off his parka in the back entryway where Mrs. Boniface kept eggs and egg cartons and stacks of the *Herald of Holiness.* She stuck her head around the door from the kitchen as Gary flexed his fingers and worked the feeling back into them. The muscles of her face squirmed with her perpetually worried look. Strange how such a good Christian lady always looked so worried, Gary thought. Of course, she'd never gotten used to Gary, to having an Indian around the place and eating in the kitchen. Gary stamped to get the snow off his boots and the bottoms of his Levi's, and after a minute Mrs. Boniface handed him the broom to help out.

"What became of Babe? The phone's been ringing and ringing for him."

"He's got a cow down. Went to see if she's calving."

"Oh." Mrs. Boniface peered out the window, but it was too dark to see past the fence and the yellow circle thrown by the yard light. Then the phone rang in the kitchen and she went scurrying to answer it.

Gary sat down on the straight-backed wooden chair in the corner of the kitchen where he always sat, smelling fried onions and potatoes and the steam from his own wool shirt. Mrs. Boniface had the telephone receiver pressed to her ear and was listening hard, her eyes roaming the kitchen until they hit Gary and glanced off. "He's real clean for a breed," he'd once heard her saying into the telephone. But he didn't give a shit about that any more, either.

"Well, I can't say when he'll be back. Gary, he tells me there's a cow down, maybe calving."

She listened intently for perhaps another minute, then straightened up like somebody'd shoved the broom handle up her. "I can't say! He's got his cow to see about, and he ain't even had his supper yet. Looks to me when a man gets voted out of public office, they shouldn't always have to be calling him away from his own business to mind theirs."

Whoever was on the other end apparently tried to argue, for Mrs. Boniface made an angry little noise and slammed the receiver down. She looked out the window for Babe, cupping her hands against the dark glass.

"It's all gonna be burned if he don't get in here pretty soon," she complained, stirring her fried potatoes. A slice of potato hopped out of the frying pan and fell on the linoleum in a whitening circle of grease. Mrs.Boniface picked it up and peered sharply at it before she dropped it back into the pan. "It just burns me up," she fretted on. "The time Babe put into that office, letting his ranch take care of itself! And after everything, they voted him out. And Babe was a good sheriff!"

Her eyes darted at Gary as if she expected him to argue with her, although Gary never said anything. "He did his job! Those that thought he was too hard on their precious brats, they should have seen to it their kids behaved, so the sheriff didn't have to be hard on them. If Babe and me'd had kids, we'd have seen they minded!"

The back door opened and Babe lumbered into the kitchen, a blast of cold air at his back. "Looks like I'm gonna have to pull that calf," he told Gary through cold-stiffened lips. "You come give me a hand. I'm gonna try to get her on the stoneboat and haul her up to the shed."

"Your supper!" wailed his wife. "And George Fiske, he keeps calling, wants you to call him back—"

"What's George want?"

She pursed her lips, her satisfaction in having news to deliver warring with her annoyance at the new sheriff. "Wants your help, of course! First he takes your office away from you and then he comes crying for help. Somebody's kidnapped the Abber baby, that's what, stole him right out of their car, and George Fiske don't know the first thing to do—" she broke off, satisfied with their reaction to her news.

"Shelley's baby?" said Gary.

It was taking a long time to soak into Babe. His pellet eyes were blank and out of focus in the big pink face that had earned him his nickname. "They sure?" he said at last.

"Are they sure? What else could happen to a baby that age, only a month old? You think he run off? You think they just misplaced him?"

"Well, Mrs. Abber, she might have come and got him.

She ain't none too happy about Shelley taking care of that first grandson, I know that."

His wife's mouth pinched at the corners until her cheeks bulged like a pocket gopher's on the way to his hole. "Mrs. Abber is under sedation. Collapsed when she heard about it. After everything she's had to stand from that girl—anyway, the rest of them, Bunch Abber and Billy and Shelley, they're at the sheriff's office now. And George, he wants you to come in. To tell him what to do next, I suppose."

Babe just stood there with the snow melting and dripping off his coat, while his wife waited by the stove, holding up her fork like it was a weapon, her mouth pinched shut and her eyes popping with what she wasn't saying.

"Well, hell," said Babe at last. "I got to get that cow in the shed, first thing I do."

Gary pulled his old Air Force parka back on and dug his gloves out of the pocket. They were still cold from before. He could hear Mrs. Boniface talking to herself as he followed Babe out into the snow.

The snow was mounding higher all the time. Much later and Gary would never have seen that dark lump down by the highway, and the cow couldn't have been missed until morning. When Gary jumped down off the stoneboat and walked around to see how she was, he could tell by the tractor lights that she had been in labor a long time. Her eyes were rolled back with fatigue and her shaggy winter hair was driven full of snow that had melted from her body heat and frozen again. A pink balloon of matter had inflated under her tail, and beneath it the snow was honeycombed and darkened with slime.

"If she could just have decided to calve before this damn storm blew in," Babe grunted. He brought a log chain from the stoneboat and fastened it around the cow's hind legs. She hardly flinched. It seemed to Gary that she was so preoccupied with what she was doing, or maybe so far gone, that she hardly knew men were fooling around with her. Natural process, except that she'd had a big Chianinna calf put in her with frozen sperm and now it was too big for her to get it out. Natural process, natural, females of every kind went through it, even human females, even

Shelley, whose breasts had been as sharp and unblemished as the glossy breasts on a center-fold girl and who had felt like wet satin up between her legs.

He shut his eyes because he didn't want to see the laboring cow and think of Shelley the way she had looked late last summer, the only time he'd seen her since he'd been back from Nam. He'd been in town with his paycheck in his pocket, about to cross the street between the Stockman's and the Vet's Club, and there was Shelley waiting on the blistering pavement outside Woolworth's for Billy's mother.

"Hi, Gary," she had said.

He'd hardly known her. She had big blue marks under her eyes and her breasts sagged like udders against her cotton maternity top. Her stomach, swollen out in front of her with Billy's baby, made her stand clumsily. Only her slim calves, immature as an eighth grade girl's, were still the same. She had stood there in the blistering heat, looking Gary in the face from a few feet away, and he had muttered *hello* and fled. Later he'd heard she had a boy.

"Wake up and give me a hand, can't you?"

They used the tractor to haul the dead weight of the cow up on the stoneboat, and then they rehitched the tractor to the stoneboat and eased back over the snow and frozen manure to the shed. Stoneboat and all, Babe hauled her inside the shed and turned off the tractor. The quiet was so sudden that Gary could hear a truck changing gears on the highway and the thick breathing of the old cow. The yellow cast from the single light bulb turned Babe's face to putty as he shucked out of his coat. "Might be she could have it by herself if I can turn it around."

Gary looked and saw that a pair of split hoofs were protruding from under the pink balloon. So the calf was coming ass backwards, like so many of those Chianinna calves. Behind him Babe had hung his mackinaw and shirt on a nail and was teeth-chattering in his undershirt. Babe's chest was doughy and fleeced with white hairs. A dewlap of skin hung down from both armpits, staining the undershirt yellow, but Babe's arms were still grizzled and stout, ending in the great meaty hands that Gary had seen pull a kid called Pat Stays Alone out of the cab of a truck and throw him against the fender so hard he bounced off. Pat had picked himself up, bleeding from the mouth, and Babe had reached out with one of those bearlike paws and clouted him along the head. Pat had gone down on the gravel and stayed there. Babe had whipped around, light on his feet for a fat man, to meet all hundred and thirty pounds of Gary Jeanmaire coming at him on a dead run; caught him in the stomach with one fist and in the face with the other. Nobody'd given a damn. It wasn't until Babe worked over one of the Pike kids, who were cousins of the Abbers, that people had gotten riled and talked George Fiske into running for county sheriff against Babe. But all that was while Gary was still in Vietnam. He and Pat had had to choose between enlisting and getting charged with illegal possession and attacking an officer of the law. They had enlisted, and Pat hadn't come back.

The cow heaved, her legs jerking spasmodically in her effort. Her belly knotted. Slime and reddened urine ran into the straw under her, but the calf's hoofs did not move. Babe went around behind her and got down on his knees, moving carefully on his rheumatic joints. Gary saw him take hold of the pair of hoofs and force them slowly back up the birth canal. Babe's hand disappeared with them, and his wrist. His arm was up the cow to his elbow; he was stretched out with his head almost on her flank, eyes intent on what he wasn't seeing as he groped inside her.

His eyes focused all at once. "Believe the old bitch has twins in her!"

He leaned back, withdrawing his arm. It was bloody and festooned with gobs of matter. "Can't budge it. Son of a bitch is gonna strangle in there and block the other one. Something else ain't right in there—can't figure it. Gimme that there rope, we'll see what we can do from this direction."

They tied the rope to the hoofs and pulled. Nothing happened. The cow kicked weakly in reflex and bawled into the straw—"Baw—aw—aw" as if they were dragging the sound out of her with her calf. Watery green manure gushed out with the birth fluids and steamed in the straw.

"Hell," panted Babe. He bent over double and puffed

with his hands braced on his knees. "Okay, give 'er another try. Lean into it, now—*heave!*"

They heaved together in silent strain. The blood ran into Gary's face until the interior of the shed darkened. The only sounds in the shed were the anguished pants of the cow, the scrape of her body being jarred and jerked backward on the rope, and the grunts of the young man and the old man as they heaved and labored.

"Heave!" They gave a mighty and concerted heave. The calf was moving down the birth canal; their momentum carried them backwards against the wall of the shed, still hauling on the rope. There was a great wrench like the sound of ripping fabric, a rush and gurgle of fluids, and the calf slid out on the straw.

"Son of a bitch!" gasped Babe. He was all in.

Gary stood up and went to look at the calf. The first thing he noticed was that it was still alive, twitching inside the swathing of bloody tissues, but something was wrong with it, and it was a long minute before it dawned on him what it was.

"Jesus Christ, look at it!"

The rage in Gary's voice caught Babe unaware. He stared slack jawed, then turned to look where Gary was looking.

"What the hell—" he began, puzzled as Gary had been.

Gary strode over to the tractor and began to rummage through the toolbox, clanging screwdrivers and bolts in his urgency.

"What're you doing?" said Babe. He stopped between Gary and the calf, his face gone flabby with perplexity. "What've you got that wrench out for?"

"What the hell you think?" Gary flared back. He was bent at the waist as if from cramps, a big crescent wrench in his hand. "Can't you see that thing's still alive? I'm gonna knock it on the—head."

"Hell, Gary, don't do that." Babe looked deflated with the effort of the birth. His upper arms and chest were blue and goose-pimpled from cold.

Gary's ears were pounding as loud as if the tractor had been fired up again in the confines of the shed. The blood in his eyes darkened the shed walls and Babe and the old cow, now heaving herself up on uncertain legs. He could taste the rage, like metal, in his throat. "You son-of-a-bitch, can't you see nothing? That thing's got two heads, can't you see? You and all the rest of your goddamn kind, you have to fuck things up, you can't let nothing alone with your goddamn artificial insemination, fucking around and fuck—fuck—" He stopped because his tongue had gotten behind his stream of thought and because he had suddenly remembered the flight of the wild geese.

Babe's face was nearly tied in a knot in his effort to figure out what Gary was talking about. "I never inseminated her, she was that way when I bought her. What's the matter with you?"

"Nothing's the matter with me that some shit like you didn't do to me! Goddamn white son-of-a-bitchin' prick with a badge on your shirt, beating up on Indian kids because you were afraid to screw around with the whites—" And that recalled more grievances, deeply buried. "You couldn't be satisfied with that, you had to kill off the tribes and screw up what was left and hog the best land—and start some frig-assed war to ship me and Pat off to—" to his fury he began stuttering again.

"You're nuts," said Babe, baffled. "I never killed no tribes. What the hell you talking about? Come on, put that wrench down. What do you want to kill that calf for, anyway? It'll likely be dead before morning."

"Because it's a goddamn fucking monster, that's why," Gary screamed. His throat was raw with the need to puncture Babe's thick skin of incomprehension. "Look at it, can't you, *look at it!*"

Babe turned obediently and stopped.

"Look there," he said. "She's motherin' it."

The old cow had tottered to her feet, afterbirth still dripping in a gob of bloody tissue from her uterus, and found her calf. She nuzzled it, stripping the birth sac away from first one head and then the other so it could breathe. Gary watched with Babe as she worked at the sodden orange fur with her tongue, coaxing the thing she had delivered to stay in the world of the living. The calf began to take shape out of the formless purplish heap it had been, and Gary could see that the two heads were joined at the base of the shoulder. The calf had two normal front legs and two rudimentary ones dangling just behind them. Incredibly, both heads moved, breathing. One eye was open, an ordinary milky-blue newborn's eye, white-lashed.

The wrench hung like a dead weight in Gary's hand, but the moment to use it had passed. He stared down at the wrench, hanging there like an extension of his forearm, a rusted metal finger with a mean head. He was trying to maintain his rage, but it kept slipping away like wisps of gauze no matter how he snatched after it.

"Don't know when I ever seen you get so mad, Gary," said Babe. His voice was relief soaked. "Made me think of the way you used to be before you joined the Air Force."

Gary looked at him. The dirty light made an old man out of Babe, turning his fact to putty and his skin to dead yellow wrinkles. Damned old fool, Gary told himself, hasn't put his shirt back on. His mouth was dry.

"Hell, I know I used to be hard on you boys. Maybe harder than I needed to be. Thing was, at times I was looking for somebody to pound on. Mrs. Boniface, she's a good Christian lady and all, but she ain't—*you* know." A flaccid eyelid dropped in a wink. "Hell, Gary, I always thought of you boys like my own. Wanted you to grow up right."

"Do all that to your own—jerk them out and beat hell out of them and ship them off to get their asses shot off—"

Babe laughed. "Now that's not how it was. Listen. Plenty of people wondered how come you hired on to work for me, after everything. Guess they wondered how I'd ever trust you. But for me, it was like having my own come back." His eyes grew soft, fixed on Gary. "That's how it was for you, too. Right? Like my own son coming back."

The words were falling all around Gary. He tried again to whip up his shelter of wrath.

"You're nuts yourself," he managed to croak. "I came to work for you because it was all the job I could find."

The door of the shed opened and Mrs. Boniface stuck her head in. She had tied a snarled wool scarf around it.

"George Fiske called again," she complained. Then she

saw Babe and gave a little shriek. "What's the matter? Where's your shirt?"

Babe reached foolishly for his shirt, as if he had forgotten it. "What's the matter with George?"

"Something about that Abber baby. He don't think it was a kidnapping, thinks you might be able to get something more out of Shelley. Wants you to come into town, first thing in the morning." She let the door of the shed close behind her. "You ask me, Shelley did something to that baby. I never thought that kidnapping story sounded right. She claimed she stopped the car at the crossroads store to buy a pack of chewing gum and when she came back out to the car, the baby was gone. But nobody else seen any traffic, and—" Just then she noticed the calf and yelped again. "What's the matter with it?"

"Don't get all het up," Babe told her, putting on his coat. "Likely be dead by morning."

"Too bad." Her eyes were avid. "I betcha we could sell it to a carnival."

Gary half-listened to her as she chattered about Shelley, what a trial the girl had been to Mrs. Abber, and what an unnatural mother, often letting her baby cry while she sat and looked at it like she had no idea what it was. Shelley, who had once slipped her hand into Gary's, trusting as a six-year-old, and looked up at him, and the expression in her eyes, what she expected him to give, had made him panic.

He rode into town in the truck with Babe the next morning to help shovel their way out to the road where the highway crews had been through with the snowplows. And he was with Babe afterward, driving ten miles east of the crossroads store with half a dozen other cars following. George Fiske, the coroner, Bunch Abber and Billy. And a few of the curious. It had taken Babe, the fearsome sheriff of her childhood, to force the account from Shelley.

Gary sat in the cab of the truck and watched Babe cross the road, hitching his coat up against the wind and taking a quick look at the horizon for the next Canadian cold front that was supposed to be on its way. Babe got down in the ditch and squatted by the entrance to the culvert, stiff in the knees as he had been the night before. He peered inside the culvert. Then he pulled his gloves out of his coat pocket and worked one on his right hand, taking time to fit all the fingers. He stuck his right arm into the culvert, all the way to the shoulder, and for a moment appeared to grope. His face was intent in the way a man's face is when he is concentrating not on the snow and frozen weeds and the road in front on him, but on what he cannot see. Then he got hold of what he was groping for and drew out his arm. The men in the other cars jumped out of their heated seats and ran to look.

"Can't figure it," one of them said as they hurried past the truck where Gary huddled. "She must be some kind of freak. She must be wrong in the head to do such a thing. Can you figure it?"

I just wanted to put it back! Shelley had wept.

Gary jumped out of the overheated cab, but he turned away from the knot of men standing around the frozen blue bundle. It seemed to him more comprehensible to put it back than to bring monsters into the world. He turned and began to walk down the snow-swept highway. Ahead of him were miles of snow-covered prairie and the invisible Sweetgrass Hills.